BENEFICIAL LIFE

STELLA ADAMS

Library of Congress Control Number: 2018903824

Fiction: Contemporary

ISBN: 978-0-9960058-21

Published by Stella Adams Printed in the USA, First Edition - Paperback and Electronic

DEDICATION

To all who have loved and lost.

Chapter One

Baltimore, Maryland 1955....

Helena Sinclair had finally come to the conclusion that time really did fly or somebody sped up the eternal clock. Here it was, the first Monday again, and she was in a tizzy. *Damn it! They come around too fast. I can't keep up with 'em,* Helena mumbled to herself as she rifled through her two church pocketbooks and tossed them on her bed with the linings hanging out. She dropped to her knees and scoured the space under the bed only to find a collection of dust. *Oh Lord,* she thought, *got to clean that out before Russell sees it. He'll have a fit. Don't know if somebody under there is coming or going,* she joked and chuckled to herself. *Out of the dust, we were created and back to the dust we return.*

Still smiling at her own joke, Helena got up off her knees, worried she wouldn't find what she sought and desperately needed. She walked over to the window of her small bedroom where a pile of Russell's grimy work clothes lay in the corner for her to wash. She knew her effort would be in vain, but she picked up each pair of pants and turned the pockets inside out, to no avail. There wasn't a nickel to be found anywhere. *Not even a lousy five cents in any of his pockets!* But she wasn't too surprised. Russell rarely took money—much less had money to take—to work. He didn't buy lunch—Helena packed sandwiches in his metal lunch box and coffee in his thermos—and he rode to work with Mose Turnbull, who he settled his transportation tab with on pay day.

Tossing the pants aside, she bolted down the stairs to the closet under the steps where she frantically searched the pockets of all the jackets hanging there—nothing. She scurried to the front room and started rummaging under the heavy pillows of the sofa and armchairs. *Voila´.* Her slim fingers touched cool metal.

Excited, Helena fished the object from the chair and held it up. *A lost earring! How did that get here? I've been looking for this earring. Thank you, Lord, but I was looking for a nickel this time,* she thought as she slumped down on the chair. Then a light bulb went off in her head, and she practically ran the short distance to the kitchen. *There has to be—yes—three Royal Crown Cola bottles I can take back to Mr. Greenberg's store!* Each bottle was worth two cents. That would give her the five cents she needed to pay the premium on her North American Beneficial Life and Casualty Insurance Company—Beneficial Life for short—insurance policy.

She picked up the bottles next to the refrigerator, grabbed her keys from the hook by the door, and headed for the corner store. While it wasn't a conscious choice, she was glad she had exited the back door and gone up the alley. She would have been mortified if any of her Walbrook Avenue neighbors had seen her taking bottles back to the store. Not that they didn't do it, but she'd rather not be seen engaged in the practice.

Helena was so obsessed with life insurance that she made great sacrifices to keep the monthly premium paid on the $1,000 policy she had on Russell. Life was hard enough, even with Russell working every day, but she was determined not to be destitute if, heaven forbid, Russell was to meet sudden death. She had seen it happen to family and church members all too many times. One memory was particularly vivid and sad.

At age 12, Helena was playing in her backyard, when a bloodcurdling scream came from two doors away. Her best friend, Patricia Robinson, came running up the alley and burst through her gate, crying, "My daddy's dead, my daddy's dead!" Not knowing what to say or do, Helena hugged Patricia and cried with her. Because he was so young and his death so sudden, Mr. Robinson's funeral was a heavy, sad affair—not the usual celebration of life. Patricia told Helena she hated that people kept calling her father's death a *'home-going.'* He was not coming back to the only home she knew, and she was miserable without him.

Helena remembered the congregation and the neighbors took up a collection for Mr. Robinson's funeral because the family had no insurance. Four months later, Patricia, her two brothers, and her mother had to move to Georgia to live with relatives because they were penniless. Helena's heart was broken when her best friend moved away. They shared gut-wrenching sobs just before the taxi left for the train station. A tearful Helena ran after the taxi until her legs gave in to the futility of the pursuit. She cried for days afterwards, knowing she would never see Patricia again.

Then there were the Hamiltons farther up the street. Within days of Mr. Hamilton's death, the Sheriff put all the family's belongings out in the street. It was distressing to see all the things Mr. Hamilton had worked so hard for there in the street, subjected to the weather, curious neighbors, and thieves.

At the time, Helena didn't know what part, if any, insurance played in the events, but she heard neighbors say Mr. Hamilton's insurance policy had lapsed. She recalled a few other similar stories that had hardened her resolve to never be without the protection of insurance.

♣

Helena never talked about life insurance with Russell, and she never asked him for money for it. It was up to her to figure out how to pay the premium and keep the policy in force. She was convinced the only way she would ever have any real money was from an insurance policy. Not that she wanted anything to happen to Russell; she loved him dearly. But, just in case.

Russell and Helena were high school sweethearts and at nineteen they were sure they knew what they wanted. So a year after their high school graduation, and with their parents' blessings, they were married in 1951. Even though they had lived with her parents, the first three years had been a struggle because Russell had trouble finding a good job, and he was extremely frugal with what money they did have. In the end, it paid off. Pinching pennies had gotten them a tiny row house with the famed Baltimore marble steps in a working-class neighborhood on Walbrook Avenue in the fourth year of their marriage.

After she and Russell settled in their home, to Helena's surprise, her parents moved back to their hometown in Guilford County, North Carolina. Helena's mother, the prim and proper Madeline Wilkes, resumed her elementary school teaching career and Emmanuel, her husband, found work as an orderly at the local hospital. Instead of his wife, Emmanuel was often mistakenly identified as the teacher because, at pushing 50, the graying in his temples and mustache made him look professorial.

The Wilkes were devout Christians, but not excessively strict with their only child. Even though they were disappointed that Helena chose marriage over college, they approved of Russell and honored Helena's decision.

♣

Cradling the soda bottles in her arms, Helena slinked into the store like Mata Hari on a spy mission.

"Morning, Mr. Greenberg," she called over the counter to the balding, middle-aged man behind the counter. "I have three bottles," which she placed on the counter in front of the grocer.

"Morning, Mrs. Sinclair. Okay. I'll take six cents off your grocery bill."

"No, no sir. I'm not shopping this morning," she said, extending her hand.

"All right," Mr. Greenberg responded, then went to the cash register to fish out six pennies. Looking down over his glasses, he put them in Helena's outstretched palm. She closed her hand over the coins and left the store like a little kid with a new toy.

Back in the house, she went into the dining room, pulled out a drawer in the china cabinet where she kept the Beneficial Life premium book, and dropped five of the six pennies into an envelope containing a dollar and twenty cents. With a heavy sigh of relief, she said to herself, "Ah, let the gray-eyed monster come now. I'm safe for another month."

Helena headed up the stairs to collect the laundry she hadn't washed over the weekend, but not before glancing at herself in the mirror on the wall, opposite the steps. Smiling, she patted her hair and gave herself a critical look. She liked what she saw, and she knew the gray-eyed monster did too. He was pleasant enough, but she still did not like him very much. Liking or disliking him, she reasoned, was not worth her energy. After all, he was only there once a month to collect for her policy. Nevertheless, she always got him out of the house as fast as she could, ignoring his predictable, hackneyed attempt at small talk.

Halfway up the stairs, the doorbell rang. *He's a little early,* she thought, retreating down the steps. A little flustered, she went to the door with a plastered smile.

"Good morning, Mrs. Sinclair," Evan Monahan, who proclaimed himself to be one of Beneficial Life's top salesman, said with his usual cheesy grin.

"Morning, Mr. Monahan," Helena replied without looking directly at the tall, lanky, white man with dark brown hair and gray-blue eyes. Reluctantly, she invited him in. "Just a minute while I get the book and the money. You can have a seat."

She quickly returned from the dining room and handed the book and life insurance payment to Evan.

"Thank you, Mrs. Sinclair," he said, taking them from her. "You know, you're one of my best customers."

"So, you've told me many times."

Laughing nervously, he replied, "Sorry. Hate to repeat myself."

Yeah, but you always do. "Quite all right, Mr. Monahan. Uh, I have work to do, and I know you have other customers to see." With that, she showed him to the door. "See you next month."

"Of course. See you next month." He exited the house and headed to his car.

Chapter Two

Evan Monahan drove his modest three-year old Ford Fairlane to the end of the shrub-lined, brick driveway of his Roland Park home and parked on the side of the house. The adjacent lawn was well cared for. A ring of tea roses grew around a tulip magnolia tree in the middle of the landscape. Bordering the edge of the lawn were brilliant green azalea bushes that had shed their lavender and white flowers, while blue hydrangeas grew along the foundation of the house. The car, which belied Evan's true social status, helped him maintain the appearance of a low-level insurance salesman.

When he turned the key in the massive oak front door and walked in, he was greeted by his lithe and graceful Abyssinian cat, Lena. The cat had been a gift, and as soon as Evan saw her, her elegance immediately reminded him of someone who occasionally plagued his thoughts. He had named the cat in honor of her—Helena Sinclair.

Lena purred as she brushed up against him. He glanced through his mail, threw his keys on the mahogany table in the entrance hall and, with Lena in tow, headed for the sunroom. His shoes thudded softly as he made his way across the marble foyer.

"Good afternoon, Mother," Evan said, as he leaned over to kiss his dozing mother on the forehead. Maureen Monahan was dark like her son, with brown eyes and brown hair. Though, Evan had his father's gray-blue eyes.

"Aw, Evan," Mrs. Monahan said, adjusting her shawl and closing her book. "You're home a little early today, aren't you? I'll never understand why you insist on doing that God-awful job of collecting money. You must go into some unsavory neighborhoods and unkempt homes," his mother whined.

"Please, Mother. Must we go over that same old, tired, ground again? If I want to take over the company when Father is gone, I'd like to know it from the ground up. Okay? That's my choice. Please give it a rest!"

"Don't count on it. And don't talk to your old mother like that!" Mrs. Monahan responded, only half seriously.

"Yes, old mother. I hope you haven't been in that chair all day!" he replied, flopping down on a rattan sofa next to her.

"Of course not," she said, picking up her book again. "We're having lamb for dinner."

"Don't hold dinner for me. I'm going out for a drink with Chaz."

"Drinking on a Monday night?"

"Mother, my thirst doesn't know the days of the week," he replied, a little annoyed.

"Why not a date with a young lady?"

"Here we go again. I have plans for a date this weekend. What you mean is, 'Why aren't you married?'" Evan retorted. "It'll happen when it happens."

"You've gone out with some lovely girls. I can't understand why nobody's caught your eye."

"Plenty have caught my eye, Mother, but none have struck my fancy!"

"Oh, please, Evan! That's a distinction without a difference. You know what they're saying about you, don't you?"

"Yes, and I don't give a damn!" an angry Evan shot back as he got up off the sofa. "See you later, Mother," he called over his shoulder, exiting the sunroom. He headed for the winding staircase in the center of the hall and went to his room.

Evan was the sole heir to the substantial insurance empire his father, Connor Monahan III had built from the ground up. His mother had refused to make her son the fourth Connor and named him *'Evan'* instead, after her own father. It didn't hurt that Connor III had inherited a small fortune from Connor Jr's rum-running escapades.

With so much at stake, Evan was leery of the women who expressed a romantic interest in him. He feared it was about his money and not about him. Much to their chagrin, he enjoyed their attention and their favors, but never took them seriously.

Once in his room, Evan stripped down to his underwear, tossed his Sears Roebuck shirt and pants across the valet chair, and flung himself on his bed. The modest clothes were also a part of the charade he was playing. The only exception to the bogus attire was the butter soft Italian loafers, which he refused to give up. He suspected his clients either didn't notice, didn't appreciate their value, or thought them to be the extravagant vice of an insignificant insurance salesman.

With his arms folded behind his head, he stared at the ceiling and wondered what it would be like to date a colored girl. *That'll be the day! Talk about being disowned! Ha! That'll be me. I guess I don't really mean date ...* With that, he drifted off to sleep, thinking about Helena Sinclair.

♣

Awakening from his nap, Evan showered, dressed, and left the house quietly. He climbed into a 1955 Corvette Stingray parked behind the house on a cement parking pad and eased his way down his tree-lined street, heading south toward downtown. Nearing his destination, he down-shifted and drove slowly through Baltimore's famed "Block." During the first half of the 20th century, the area had contained famous burlesque houses, but had now given way to even seedier strip clubs and sex shops.

On these trips, Evan never got out of the car. He was afraid of the element that hung out there, but took great pleasure in cruising the area and taking in the sights. The streetwalkers in their garish make-up and skimpy, cheap clothes excited him. What excited him most was the rare sighting of a colored girl—of any hue. He was mesmerized by the variations in skin color and he named them—caramel, honey, almond, chocolate, molasses, coffee, walnut, ebony, and topaz. He fantasized about touching one of them and wondered what they might feel like—silk, Italian leather, or just plain old skin. He didn't know, but he was aroused thinking about it.

Evan stopped at the light at the intersection of Baltimore and Gay streets, and out of the shadows a slightly over-weight, voluptuous platinum blond woman in stilettos approached the car and leaned into the open window. She smelled of cheap perfume and stale cigarettes. Evan was taken aback by her approach and recoiled slightly at the scent of her.

"Hey handsome," she said in a coarse, whiskey voice. "How about some fun tonight?"

Slightly nauseous from the stench, he barked, "Step away from the car, lady!" and sped off.

What was I thinking? he asked himself as he maneuvered the car through the intersection. He had never entertained the idea of actually being with any ladies of the night. For him, the fantasy of it all was better than the reality. He had friends who bragged about their encounters with prostitutes on the block, but he knew he'd never stoop so low and besides, why would he pay for it when he could get it for free? He managed to have some relationships with no strings and no emotional attachments.

Evan pulled into the parking lot of O'Doulie's Pub, his favorite Irish watering hole, hoping to find his good friend, Chaz, inside. As he entered the smoked-filled room, he paused to let his eyes adjust to the dimly lit room, and then craned his neck to look for Chaz.

"Evan, over here," came a familiar voice. Charles "Chaz" Hildebrandt, a law clerk for a state supreme court judge, had movie star good looks – natural blond hair, blue eyes, chiseled features and a row of white teeth that were as even as tombstones in Arlington National Cemetery. Sometimes Evan hated him for being so handsome, but not for long because Chaz was a genuinely nice guy.

Making his way to the sound of his name, Evan greeted Chaz with a slap on the back. "Hey buddy. See you started without me."

"Ev, old man. Wasn't sure you were going to make it. Have a draft," Chaz said, raising his hand to signal the bartender. "Looks like you could use one.

You look a little green around the gills. You sick or something?"

"Sick? Me? No!" Some guy almost side-swiped the Stingray. Got me a little jittery."

"You serious? It's just a car Evan. Repeat after me, 'it's just a car.'"

"Yeah, I know. Excuse me a minute, I have to go to the head." And before Chaz could say anything else, Evan went into the men's room and splashed cold water on his face. After he composed himself, he went back to the bar to rejoin Chaz.

"You sure you're okay? I ordered you a Natty Boh."

"Yeah Chaz, I'm okay. Question: Have you ever dated a married woman?"

"What? You know everybody I've ever dated. And if I did, I sure wouldn't tell you. What's up with you? Whose wife are you interested in?"

"Nobody's. I was just asking."

"You're lying. Who is she? Nobody you work with, I hope."

"Nobody I work with. I think it's an infatuation, but it's there."

"Too bad she's married. It would make your mother happy."

"Leave my mother out of this. Sorry I brought it up."

"It would even stop some of the talk."

"Like I told my mother, I don't give a damn about the talk. I'm not a faggot."

"Down boy! I know that...I guess I know that," he laughed. Why don't you take Rebecca out? You say jump and she'll say how high."

"Because she's your cousin. That's like dating your sister, which I wouldn't do."

"If I had a sister, I wouldn't *let* you date her, but my cousin...that's copasetic. What's the down-low on this married woman?"

"Not only is she married, she's...nothing. Forget it."

"What? Fat? Ugly?"

"Nothing. Forget it. Think I'll call it a night. See you buddy." With that, Evan tossed a twenty-dollar bill on the counter and slid off his stool. A bewildered Chaz called after him, but Evan, head down, kept walking, waved and left the bar. When he reached the spot where he had parked the Stingray, he leaned his back against it, pulled a pack of Marlboros from his jacket pocket and lit up. As the smoke from his cigarette swirled in the night air, Evan hoped his 'caramel infatuation' would dissipate the same way.

Chapter Three

Russell Sinclair was proud of his success at such a young age. He worked hard, spent his money carefully, and took care of his household the way his father had taught him. Born in Alabama, Russell was the youngest of five siblings, and because he was born when his parents were in their late thirties, they called him the 'oops child,' which he hated. By the time he was born, his siblings had gotten on with their lives and he hardly knew them.

His father, Nathaniel, was a farmer at heart and loved the land he had inherited from his own father and worked it as long as his health and strength had allowed. Nathaniel resisted the great migration north, but saw his oldest children shun farming and move away: the only daughter to Chicago, Illinois and three sons to Gainesville, Florida.

Russell's mother, Sadie, was a warm and loving woman who devoted her life to her five children, but she didn't want Russell tied to the farm. At twelve-years old, she sent him to live with his father's cousins in Baltimore where he was loved and raised the way she and Nathaniel would have raised him. Though he was well cared for and loved, Russell felt his parents had rejected him.

Russell turned the key, went inside his modest row house, and began his evening ritual by calling for his wife as soon as he let himself in.

"Hey baby, where are you? I'm home," he yelled per his usual after-work greeting. Sometimes Helena met him at the door, sometimes not. He didn't think it was possible to love a human being the way he loved his wife. And despite having had one miscarriage, she was talking about getting pregnant again. Where would he find the capacity to love her and a baby too? He couldn't fathom it, but the idea of a little him running around made him thump his chest. Perhaps he'd give it serious consideration, especially since Helena was getting bored at home and was talking about getting a job. On second thought, he wasn't having it. His wife was not going to work!

Russell went straight to the basement to take off his dusty construction clothes, and noticed his wife doing laundry. "Hey babe," he said, as he sneaked up behind her and encircled her tiny waist, pulling her toward him.

Helena nearly jumped out of her skin. Unintentionally, he startled her as she put laundry in the sanitary tub to soak overnight. "Russell, why do you do that? You scare me to death every time you do it," she said, as she turned to kiss him. "Now get away and take your dirty, stinky clothes off," she replied, gently pushing him away.

"Thought you washed Saturday."

"Some, but not everything. Maybe you can think about buying me a washing machine. Your work clothes are hard to clean by hand, and they're breaking my back!"

"Think about it? Sure, I'll *think* about it. But you could always go to the Laundromat," he laughed as she made a face. The ringing telephone interrupted their light banter. "I'll get it," Russell said, as he headed up the steps in a cloud of dust.

"You're making more work for me," she yelled after him, seeing the trail he left behind.

Russell picked up the phone from the server in the dining room. "Hello." Hearing the voice on the other end, he froze for a split second. "How did you get my number? Why you calling me at home?" Before the voice on the other end could say anything further, Russell slammed the phone down. Running his hands over his head, he paced until he heard Helena coming up from the cellar.

"Who was on the phone?" she asked.

"Mose. He wanted to know if I wanted to play some cards tonight," Russell responded trying to contain his anxiety.

"On a Monday night?"

"That's what I said," Russell replied, as he brushed by Helena on his way to the basement again. His voice trailed off as he went down stairs. "I still have on these dirty clothes—"

With a shrug of her shoulders and a quizzical look on her face, Helena headed for the kitchen to start dinner when the telephone rang again. As she picked it up, she heard Russell coming back up the stairs. "Hello," she said to empty air. "Hello, anybody there?" Again nothing. "Hello. Somebody say something." Still no response. Slowly placing the phone back on the cradle, she turned toward Russell. "Funny. Nobody there," she said, perplexed.

Barefoot and in his underwear, Russell headed up to the second floor to take a bath. "Wrong number I guess," he called over his shoulder, trying to contain his breathing.

"Guess so," Helena reluctantly concluded.

At dinner, Russell was noticeably distracted. Helena found herself repeating almost everything she had to say.

♣

The next morning, the alarm clock jangled at the ungodly hour of four a.m., and Russell slammed down the off button with a vengeance. Helena stirred as he got up. "Go on back to sleep," he said softly. "I'll just eat some cereal this morning."

"You sure?" a barely awake Helena replied.

"Yeah. I told you, you don't have to get up with me every morning. I've been well trained. I can even make my own coffee. Now go back to sleep," he said, patting her on the butt and heading for the bathroom.

Unbeknownst to Helena, Russell had spent most of the night staring at the ceiling, wanting to touch her but too consumed with guilt to do so. He knew he'd have a hard time at work today because he was exhausted, and he had a problem he needed to solve.

After dressing, Russell quietly went down stairs, grabbed his lunch pail, and headed out the door to wait for Mose.

Moses Turnbull, the giver of advice on every imaginable subject, was only five years older than Russell, chronologically, but light years older in street smarts, and Russell needed his help in solving his latest dilemma.

Mose pulled up to the curb in his Buick Skylark and Russell got in. Since he was the first stop, Russell had some time to talk before Mose picked up Roger and Greg, the other two riders.

"Morning, Mose. How you?"

"Anxious to get to work, ain't you? You standing on the curb. I'm shocked I didn't have to honk this morning. What, your old lady put you out?" Mose chided in his gravelly voice, a voice that invoked a presence his five-foot seven frame, albeit stocky, could not do on its own.

When Russell didn't come back with a quick retort, Mose stole a quick glance in his direction. "What's up Youngster?" he asked, calling Russell by the nickname he had given him.

"Helena didn't put me out—yet—but, she just might," Russell replied softly.

"Don't tell me you done gone and messed up your good thing! I thought you were better than that, Youngster. Leave whoever she is alone and keep it to yourself. Don't go confessin'."

"Mose, do you think you could lend me some money?"

"You gonna make me pull this car over. What you gone and done? Man, what's wrong with a raincoat when you dipping and dabbing?"

"Hold up, Mose!" Russell said, raising his hands. "Why did your mind automatically go to the gutter? No man, you got it wrong! I'm into Nipper for three hundred dollars."

"Thank God, it's not what I thought. I knew I raised you better than that!" Mose said, wiping imaginary sweat from his forehead. "But didn't I tell you about shooting craps at lunch time, especially with Nipper and his crowd? Three hundred dollars is a lot of bread, man. I ain't got that kind of money lying around. I could, maybe, spot you a yard, but I still have to talk to Clarice before I do something like that."

"I thought you were the man in your house."

"Excuse me? You not gettin' in *my* shit about *my* money and how I run *my* house are you? You ain't in no position to do that, Youngster."

"Sorry. You're right. It's just that I don't know what to do. Nipper called the house last night—I don't know how he got my number—and told me I got a week to get his money."

"Ok, maybe if you give him the yard, you can work out something for the rest to keep him from taking it out on your ass. Maybe I can talk to him."

"Thanks, but I don't want you involved in this."

"Oh, yeah? Then you shouldna asked me for my money!"

Russell fell silent as they pulled up to Roger's house.

♣

Mose's childhood in Mississippi had been a difficult one. Both sets of his grandparents had been sharecroppers, barely eking out enough to support their families. Mose's parents met on one of the local farms during harvest season, married young, and made their way north. Neither of them finished high school, and they lived from hand-to-mouth to feed the five children they ultimately had. Mose, second from the youngest, graduated from high school, but barely, and bounced from menial job to menial job until he learned to lay bricks.

Hard work and stress killed his parents before their time, but they had instilled in him a strong work ethic and left a longing for family. Unfortunately, he had little contact with his siblings, who were scattered across the country. He was the only one to move to Baltimore where he first found work on the docks, then later in construction. Baltimore was where he met Clarice Snowden, who became his common-law wife. He was instantly smitten and, not being one to stand on ceremony, moved her into his small apartment without benefit of marriage. The arrangement, scandalous in the eyes of Clarice's parents, fueled their luke-warm tolerance of Mose. Everyone else assumed they were married, and Mose had no intention of telling them otherwise. Though rarely discussed, it was a common practice. Considering his constant moralizing with Russell Sinclair, he especially wanted to keep his hypocrisy a secret from him.

Clarice was thirty, two years older than Mose, and had a thirteen-year old son, Raymond 'Ray', whose biological father she refused to identify. Mose had been willing to be a father to Ray, but the boy rejected the notion, having spent most of his life with his grandparents. It suited the grandparents just fine.

Mose had been a little surprised that Clarice didn't insist her son come live with them, but she seemed uncomfortable in his presence, perhaps because nobody could believe he was her son, especially since he was so 'bright' and Clarice was so dark. Ray reminded Mose of a ditty from his childhood in Mississippi. *Light bright, almost white, but not quite.* A practical man, he thought it best to let sleeping dogs lie. If Clarice didn't want to talk about Ray's father, that was perfectly fine by him. She apparently had good reason.

Chapter Four

At the end of the week, when Russell was leaving the job site and heading for the parking lot, he was accosted by a stylishly dressed, wiry, five-foot eleven guy wearing shades and a big apple cap, cocked to the side. Two similarly dressed, hefty henchmen flanked Russell.

"Hold up, Sinclair," Nipper said, stepping into Russell's path. "You got something for me?"

"First, you need to get out my face. But yeah, let's talk," Russell replied, taking a step backward, while keeping an eye on the men with Nipper.

"Talk?" Nipper replied with a sardonic grin. "Ain't nothing to talk about boy. Gimme my money!"

Russell looked around nervously as more construction workers, who were supposed to be on their way home, were headed in their direction.

"Don't do this here," he urged. "Let's go over to the parking lot..."

"It ain't gotta be all that," Nipper replied. "Just hand over the dough, and me and my boys will be on our way."

Nodding toward the street, Russell attempted to step around Nipper and head for the parking lot when Nipper restrained Russell by placing a heavy hand on his chest. "Where the hell do you think you're goin', motherfucker?"

A slim but muscular, six-foot-one Russell knocked Nipper's hand away, and said, emphatically, "I said let's go to the parking lot and handle this business."

By this time, one of the henchmen was resting his hand inside his jacket and staring intently at Russell. Nipper looked his way and shook his head.

"Let's go," Nipper said, grabbing Russell by the arm and leading him across the street. Russell wrenched himself free, and headed toward the lot. Stopping between a row of cars, Nipper barked, "Talk!"

"Look man," Russell began, "I can give you a yard today and give you twenty-five dollars every Friday until the rest is paid." When Russell started to go into his pocket for the money, the other henchman reached into his jacket, too.

"What I look like to you? A savings and loan company? You lost it all at one time. I want it back the same way you lost it."

27

"I know man, but I don't have it all right now," Russell explained.

"That's too bad," Nipper retorted. He caught Russell off guard and punched him in the stomach. As he doubled over in pain, Mose, Roger, and Greg appeared out of nowhere.

"Hey, Nipper!" Mose yelled in his gravelly voice. "Let me talk to you."

"What's with you niggers and talkin'? And what you got to do with it anyway?" Nipper sneered as one of the henchmen put his arm out to stop Mose.

"Look Nipper," Mose said with outstretched hands. "Youngster here didn't know what he was up against. Take the yard and let him pay you weekly."

"Are you gonna guarantee the weekly?" Nipper asked.

"Yeah, he's good for it. I'll make sure of it. Call your boys off. If he's hurt, he can't work. If he can't work, he can't pay you your money," Moses explained.

"Not a problem. He can't pay, you pay. I get my money one way or another. And I ain't worried about these clowns with you," Nipper said, sneering at Roger and Greg. "I'll see you next Friday, right here," he said as he pointed a finger toward the ground. Then he turned back to Russell and gave him another surprise punch to the gut.

Roger and Greg were about to spring into action, but Mose stopped them, figuring they were out gunned and out "hefted." Nipper and his men

28

laughed, and then beat a swift retreat across the lot to a waiting car.

Mose helped a winded Russell walk slowly to the car, while Roger and Greg walked behind; looking backwards to be sure Nipper and company actually sped away.

"Man, I'm sorry I got you guys into this." Russell winced as they climbed into the car.

"Me too!" Roger joked, lessening the tension. "But, seriously man, we got your back."

"Yeah," Mose said softly. Even when he spoke softly, he sounded intense. "Just pay your debts and stay away from Nipper."

"I got it. I'm sorry," an embarrassed and hurting Russell responded. They drove the rest of the way in silence.

♣

When Mose pulled up to Russell's house, the last stop on the return trip home, he posed the question Russell had been dreading.

"What are you going to tell Helena?"

"I don't know. Thanks to you, this week's envelope will be all right, but next week's – twenty-five dollars short is going to be hard to explain."

"No, it won't be. Just tell the truth. Helena will forgive you. She won't like it. She'll raise hell, but I think she'll forgive you."

"Forgiving me is one thing, but when the ends don't meet, that's another."

"You shoulda thought of that when you was shooting them craps. You need to come clean, Youngster."

"I know Mose. I know. But, you know what she thinks of gambling."

"You want her to think you're spending it on another woman?"

"Naw, she knows better than that—"

"Come on, Youngster. You can't be that naïve. That'll be the first thing that come to her mind. It was the first thing I thought."

"Maybe I can tell her the work at the site is winding down and they cut my hours."

"That should work! Add lying to gamblin'. Soon you'll be stealin' and whorin'."

"Why you got to exaggerate? You know me better than that."

"If you want any peace in your house, you better tell the truth and be real sorry. Or you can tell yourself what you told me, 'you the man in your house'. I guess that means you can do what you want. Try that shit and see how it works for you!"

"I'm better at poker than at craps. Maybe I can find a game and win the ..."

Throwing up his hands, Mose interrupted Russell in mid-sentence. "You need to shut up and get your head straight! Gamblin' got you in this mess, now you think gamblin's going to get you out of it? Get out of my car! And I want *my* money back just like Nipper wants his."

30

A crushed Russell turned the handle and started out of the car. "I hear you Mose—sorry. I'll figure it out." He slammed the door and, with his head hung low, walked slowly up the sidewalk. Instead of going directly into the house, he flopped down on the famed Baltimore marble steps to collect his thoughts.

Chapter Five

On Fridays, Russell usually brought his pay envelope home and put it on the dining room table—fifty-three dollars, after he took out twenty dollars and thirty-three cents he kept as pocket money. Since he wouldn't be short this week, he toyed with the idea of waiting until next week to tell Helena about his gambling debt. This was their Friday night to go to the movies—the Bridge on Edmondson Avenue or the Met on North Avenue—and he didn't want to spoil it. They went to the movies on alternating weeks. On the off movie-week, Russell got his hair cut and Helena went to the beauty parlor. When it came to money, theirs was a regimented life. Now with an unexpected debt, they would be unable to save any money for a while. What he knew for sure was there wasn't going to be a washing machine in the house any time soon. He winced at the thought of having to tell his wife the news.

Dusting some of the construction dirt from his clothes, he hesitantly went in the house. Wouldn't you know it? Helena met him at the door with a kiss.

"Hey honey. How was your day?"

Russell grunted some inaudible comment and headed for the basement.

"Excuse me, Mr. Sinclair!" Helena called after him. "What kinda way is that to greet the woman who missed you all day?"

"See," Russell called over his shoulder, "can't predict you women. You usually say, 'get away, you stink.'"

"You do stink and your attitude this week has been stinky too!"

"Sorry baby, just tired I guess."

"I got your tired," she yelled on her way up to the second floor. "Come and get it!"

Russell's stomach sunk. Any other time, just the mere suggestion of making love with his wife would send his pulse racing, but not today. He deposited his work clothes in the basket in the basement, which took no time at all, but he didn't attempt to go upstairs until Helena summoned him, fifteen minutes later.

"Russell, get up here, now!" Helena shouted. "What's taking you so long?"

He made his way slowly up the steps and went into the bathroom to find his bath already drawn and a nude, caramel-colored, five foot six, Helena sitting cross-legged on the closed commode. She was slender and long-waisted with ample breasts perched high on her chest. Her stomach was perfectly flat and her hips perfectly round, atop long, shapely legs. When she first began shaving her legs, Russell had objected loudly, but now he loved their smooth, silkiness. Surprised to see her sitting there, his body immediately responded.

"That's what I like to see," she said, getting up to kiss him. "Hurry up. I'll be down the hall waiting for you," and she sashayed out of the bathroom.

I'll wait until tomorrow to tell her about Nipper, Russell thought. Easing down into the tub, he flinched as the water stung his midsection, which he discovered was bright red from the punches he had taken at the hand of Nipper. He was afraid he might have to come clean after all. The thought deflated more than his ego.

♣

In her naiveté, Helen thought she would be able to tell if her husband was seeing another woman by his response. What else could it be? Strange phone calls and no sex all week. He'd have hell to pay. And did he have some kind of rash on his stomach?

♣

Before the next payday, Russell had reluctantly confessed his gambling losses because he knew his check would be short. Helena could have never imaged being so angry with him or that a frugal Russell would be a gambler. He knew she disapproved of gambling on moral grounds. In a more practical sense, she called it a 'fool's pastime.' They simply did not have money to waste!

"You might as well burn your next eight paychecks. That's what it amounts to!" she had shouted at the top of her lungs. She was outraged that he could waste his hard-earned money in such a way, especially when she wanted a washing machine, especially when she scrimped and saved, and the *'especiallies'* went on for several minutes with Russell unable to get a word in edgewise. Then she had hurriedly dressed and stormed out of the house. Beads of perspiration had dotted her forehead as she aimlessly walked toward North Avenue. The notion he was having an affair disappeared completely.

Now here it was the first Monday again and she had no money for the insurance man, she mused as she did the weekly ironing in her unfinished basement. Though she could not carry a tune in a bucket, she sang loudly accompanying the turquoise and beige Victrola whirling her favorite forty-five records. Depending on her mood, she crooned with the worldly soul sound of Etta James or the spiritual sound of gospel singer, James Cleveland. Today it was James Cleveland. The music got her through her tasks, and took her mind off the fact that she was broke.

Helena finished pressing the last of the stiffly starched crochet doilies that went on the arms of the living room chairs. Then she clanked the iron down on its triangular steel plate and switched off the portable heater. The basement was chilly in early spring and she could feel the cold of the linoleum rug seeping through her thin bedroom slippers. Time to head upstairs to get ready for the gray-eyed monster.

She dreaded hearing the doorbell ring, but she had no choice but to answer. "Morning, Mr. Monahan," she said, barely opening the door.

So accustomed was he to being invited in, that he started in before he realized Helena was blocking his path. "Something wrong, Mrs. Sinclair?" a very surprised Evan asked. His body language told her he still expected to be let in.

"As a matter of fact, there is Mr. Monahan," an almost tearful Helena began.

"I'm sorry to hear that. Um ... is there anything I can do? Care to tell me about it?"

"No, well yes. I guess you need to come in."

Concern and curiosity registered on Evan's face as he stepped into the house. "Just what is it, Mrs. Sinclair?"

"I don't have the premium money this month," she replied hesitantly.

"Good God, Mrs. Sinclair! I thought you had a problem! Like somebody died or something, but then you would have needed me, wouldn't you?" he laughed.

"I don't see anything funny, Mr. Monahan, and to me, it is a problem."

"I'm sorry, Helena... "Mrs. Sinclair."

Helena was too upset to notice he had called her by her first name. "Why isn't it a problem? Can you do something?"

"Yes ma'am. Sure can. You have a thirty-day grace period. So I'll come back in about three weeks—before the grace period is up—and you can pay me then. Of course, I don't want to make two trips, so it would be good if you can pay next month's premium at the same time. How does that sound?"

Her spirits lifted, Helena replied, "I didn't remember the grace period. Thank you, Mr. Monahan. That means you'll be back...."

"Let's see, today is May 2nd, so I'll come back on Friday, the 27th, just before the Memorial Day weekend. Your thirty days wouldn't be up, exactly, but it would give me time to get the paperwork in." He looked at his pocket calendar and made a note. "If you could make the June payment then, it would save me a trip."

"May I see your calendar, Mr. Monahan?" Helena asked, taking it from Evan's hand.

"Sure," a flushed Evan replied, relinquishing the calendar with the realization she had almost touched him.

"I don't know. That'll be a whole week in advance. Maybe. I can't promise you that I'll have the June payment then."

"Let's play it by ear. I guess I'll just have to make two trips," he said thoughtfully, and looked directly at Helena. "Did Mr. Sinclair get laid off or something?"

"Or something," she replied, starting for the door. "Thanks, Mr. Monahan. I appreciate you working with me on this."

Evan got the message, so turned and headed for the door. "You're welcome, Mrs. Sinclair. You're one of my best customers, you know. See you soon."

Helena closed the door behind Evan and leaned against it. *I don't know how I'm going to get that money. I could kill Russell!* Then a funny thought occurred to her, and she smiled. *I better do it before the insurance lapses!*

Chapter Six

White-hot pain coursed through Helena's body as she tried to get out of bed. Her lips mouthed her husband's name but no sound came out. "Russell, Russell," she cried, doubled over with pain. She pulled the sheet with her as she slid out of bed and dropped to her knees, hoping Russell would feel a sudden chill and wake up. "Russell, Oh God, Russell," she moaned, barely audible.

Russell stirred then patted the other side of the bed, unconsciously feeling for Helena. It took a moment for him to connect the empty space with the groaning he heard. In one motion, he slid out of bed and switched on the lamp on the nightstand. As he rounded the bed, tripping over the bathrobe he had carelessly dropped the night before, he found his wife curled up on the floor, blood running down her leg. "Helena," he said, gathering her in his arms and rocking her. "What is it? We need to get you to the hospital. I'll call a cab."

Shaking her head, Helena responded, "No, call Natalie. She'll get here faster." Then she began to sob, loud, gut wrenching sobs. "The baby—I lost the baby."

"Shh, honey, shh," Russell said, as he scooped her off the floor and deposited her softly on the bed.

Picking up the phone, he called Natalie, Helena's best friend, who only lived two blocks away and who was lucky enough to have an old beat up jalopy.

A sleepy Natalie picked up the phone. "Hello? It's three o'clock in the morning. This better be good," she mumbled.

"Natalie, it's me, Russell. Can you get here quick? Helena is losing the baby—"

"Russell? Baby?" Natalie responded, sitting up in the bed. "I didn't know she was—"

Russell cut her off. "Me neither. Can you come?"

"On my way!"

♣

Russell rushed through the emergency doors of Provident Hospital, Baltimore's only private Negro hospital, carrying his wife in his arms. "I need help here! Somebody help!"

A white-uniformed nurse in a stiff starched RN cap met him. "What's the problem, sir?" she asked, putting her hand on Helena's forehead.

Running from the parking lot, an out-of-breath Natalie yelled as she burst through the doors. "Can't you see she's hemorrhaging?"

"Calm down, miss," the stern nurse said quietly but firmly. "Follow me, sir," she said, as she walked down the hall and showed Russell to an empty exam room. As she passed the nurses' station, she barked orders to the aide sitting there. "See if an OB/GYN is in the building!"

The likelihood of that was slim. Specialists were never routinely on duty in the ER, and Obstetricians and Gynecologists made their rounds earlier in the day. By dinnertime, they were usually long gone. A staff doctor was on call for those women who did not have a private physician when it came time to deliver.

Russell gingerly laid Helena on the gurney. "Can't you call her doctor? She's having a miscarriage!"

"Just a minute, sir. How far along is—was she?"

"I don't know," Russell stammered.

"You don't know?" the incredulous nurse asked with a raised eyebrow.

Raising her head, Helena said, "About six weeks. Call Doctor Lewis Hill, please."

The nurse pushed the intercom button on the wall. "Assistance is needed in room six. Assistance in room six." Then she turned to Russell, "Sir, you need to go to the desk and register your wife while I get her vitals and call Dr. Hill. The ER doctor will see her in the meantime." She dismissed Russell with a flick of her hand and started taking Helena's vitals.

♣

In the waiting room, Natalie sat flipping through an Ebony magazine while Russell's nodding head rhythmically banged on the wall behind his chair. After they had waited two hours, Dr. Hill, an amicable, fortyish man of West Indian descent, came to give them an update.

"Hi Doctor," Russell said, standing up and extending his hand. "How is she?"

"Good Morning, Mr. Sinclair. Fine. She'll be fine. As you know, she had a miscarriage. While that's unfortunate, medically it's common, though not normal. You understand what I mean?" Seeing Russell nod, he continued. "She lost a fair amount of blood, but she'll be all right. Since it was early, there is no need for a D&C. We will keep her overnight for observation. She may be a little weak and light-headed, but she'll be okay."

"Dr. Hill. Had she been to see you? I didn't even know—"

"That's something you have to discuss with your wife, Mr. Sinclair. But I will tell you this - you know this is her second miscarriage, so I need to see you both in the office to talk about future pregnancies. The nurse will come out and let you know when you can see your wife."

"Yes, sir," Russell responded, biting his lip. He dropped his head as if he were to blame for this turn of events.

Dr. Hill patted Russell on the forearm and left the way he came. "See you soon."

♣

Returning from Dr. Hill's office a week later, they didn't speak during the taxi ride home. The tension between them could be cut with the proverbial knife. Once at home, Russell unlocked the door and let Helena in ahead of himself. Still silent, she headed for the stairs with Russell close behind. Without warning, Russell grabbed her by the arm and spun her around so hard she landed hard against his chest. He held her in a firm grip. "I still don't see why you didn't tell me you were going to have a baby. I don't understand that at all."

"Let me go, Russell," she said between clenched teeth.

"No! How do you think I felt when Dr. Hill was the one to tell me? I felt like a fool. Why were you keeping it from me?"

"I wasn't keeping it from you. I just hadn't got around to telling you."

"I repeat, why?" he said, raising his voice slightly and not loosening his hold on her. "I hope to hell you weren't planning to do something stupid!"

"You know me better than that," Helena responded, trying to wiggle free. "It's just that I—

we've—been so worried about money lately, I didn't want to—"

Russell took a step back and looked Helena directly in the eye. "That makes no sense. I was going to know sooner or later, so what did money have to do with it? Besides, what happened to 'God will provide?' You're the one with all the faith. You're still mad at me! That's what it is. I'm sorry. How many ways can I say it? Helena, don't do this to me. I love you. I made a mistake."

Her whole body melted into his. "I know Russell. I'm just a worrier. Yeah, I'm still a little upset, but I wasn't going to do anything to myself—or the baby. I was just scared I would lose it and I didn't want you to blame yourself. Even though Dr. Hill said stress isn't good, he said it wasn't the reason for the miscarriage."

"I heard him, and I don't think you're buying it," Russell said, stroking her hair, "which makes me feel guilty."

"A little guilt is good. Maybe you'll think twice next time—"

Exasperated, he released her, took a deep breath and threw up his arms. "Not another lecture about gambling."

She immediately grabbed his arms and put them back around her waist. "We'll get through this," she whispered tilting her head back for a kiss.

Russell bent down to meet her lips. "We will—but I don't know about this rhythm method. Seems awful complicated to me…tracking menstrual history so we'll know when you're fertile."

"Yeah but leave it to me. Dr. Hill explained it to me. According to him, women are only fertile for a short time each month, so we have to avoid that time. He showed me how to figure it out."

"Like I said. Complicated."

"Take your pick. It's either raincoats—which you hate—or abstinence."

"Get real, girl."

"Okay. Rhythm it is."

Chapter Seven

Muttering to himself, Mose honked his horn and waited for Russell. The house was dark, signaling that Helena was probably still asleep, or at least still in bed. After a few minutes, Russell ambled out the door and down the steps. "Morning," he mumbled, getting into the car.

Mose responded with a grunt and pulled away from the curb. He waited a few minutes, then asked, "How's Helena doing these days?"

"Okay. All she needed was a day or two off her feet. Her doctor just didn't want her doing steps for a while. Natalie stayed with her and fixed her lunch and stuff. Now that she's had a couple of weeks of taking it easy, she's just fine."

"Clarice says y'all may have to wait awhile for that baby."

"That's none of Clarice's business. Women talk too much. Really it ain't nobody's business."

"You been awfully touchy lately, Youngster. And you always saying something about Clarice." When Russell didn't respond, Mose continued, feigning indignation. "What's your damn problem? I was just concerned about you and your wife. That's what friends are about. You ain't been cut off long enough to be so stressed," Mose said with a knowing grin.

"See, Mose, you don't know when to quit. I draw the line at my bedroom. Okay?"

"Yeah, yeah. Pardon my round shoulders. Better yet, kiss my ass," he laughed to reduce the tension he sensed building in Russell. He headed toward Greg's house, which was usually the last pick-up.

"What? No Roger this morning?" Russell asked.

"Naw. He said he'll take the bus for a while and maybe even find another ride."

"What?" a surprised Russell responded. "What's his problem?"

"You," Mose responded, reaching in his shirt pocket for a cigarette.

Russell turned in his seat to look at Mose. "Me! Me? What did I do to him?"

"You didn't do nothing. Well, not exactly. He don't want your trouble with Nipper to rub off on him, so he thought he'd keep his distance."

"So much for having my back. I don't need him anyway. I got Nipper handled."

47

"I hear you, Youngster. Make sure you ain't just blowing smoke."

Chapter Eight

Helena stood at the front room window, waiting and looking for the gray-eyed monster. It was May 27th and she dreaded this Friday's visit more than any of the other first Mondays she could remember. Before long, Evan Monahan pulled up and parked in front of the row home. Helena watched him gather some things from the front seat and pause a moment before he climbed out of the car. As he walked up the sidewalk, she noticed there was something different about him. She wasn't sure what, but thought it could be his hair. It was combed differently, and he didn't have his glasses on, which made him look a lot less corny. *Curious,* she thought, but dismissed it.

As he approached the door, she went to intercept him, and before he could ring the bell, she opened the door to find a grinning Evan.

"Good Morning, Mrs. Sinclair," he said with a nod of his head.

Helena nodded her head in return, and did not say a word. She stepped aside and motioned for Evan to come in.

"I hate to tell you this, Mr. Monahan, but you made the trip for nothing," she began.

"Oh? Why do you say that?" Evan said, taking the liberty to sit on the sofa, though he had not been invited to do so.

"I simply do not have the money for last's month's premium or this month's, for that matter," she said, saddened by the fact, but miffed when Evan leisurely stretched his long legs out in front of him and rested his hands behind his head as if he had come for a social call. She glared down at him and couldn't help but notice the expensive looking loafers he wore. Momentarily distracted, she lost her train of thought.

Evan immediately filled in the awkward silence. "I'm sorry to hear that, Helena," he began. "I don't know what I can do."

She frowned. *Helena? Helena? Did he just call me by my first name?* "I've been a good customer for over a year, MR. MONAHAN," she replied, placing great emphasis on his surname. "Maybe not good enough to call you by your first name, but—"

50

Casually getting up from the sofa, Evan stared at Helena with the look in his eyes that she loathed. She took two steps backwards and averted his gaze.

"Let's see," he said. "On second thought, I do have a little bit of pull with the company. I didn't get to be the top salesman for nothing." He reached inside his jacket pocket, pulled out a small note pad and tore a sheet of paper from it. "I'll write an I.O.U. for two dollars and fifty cents, which will cover you for May and June. All you have to do is sign it, and pay me back when you can," he said, handing Helena the paper and pen.

"I don't know," Helena began hesitantly. "I don't want to be in your debt."

"What choice do you have? Either your insurance lapses or you owe me."

Me? Did he say what I thought he said! At that, Helena folded her arms and shot him a hot glare.

Evan changed his tone. "Please don't worry about owing me. I know you'll pay as soon as your situation—whatever it is—straightens out." He continued to hold the I.O.U. in one outstretched hand and the pen in the other.

Worried silly about losing their life insurance, Helena reluctantly took the pen and paper and signed her name. For some reason, she felt like she had just made a deal with the devil.

"Don't worry, Hel—Mrs. Sinclair. You did the right thing. It would be a shame to lose all the money you've already invested." Evan fished his wallet from his back pocket, took the paper from Helena, folded it and tucked it inside. Helena could not help noticing the quality of Evan's wallet matched that of his shoes. *How much do insurance men make?* she wondered.

"How much time do I have?" she inquired.

"Time? Oh, you mean to repay? I told you, don't worry. How about the end of the year? December is good. Okay?"

"December? Yes," Helena replied. That seemed reasonable enough. Nipper would be paid, and she hoped to have landed a job by then. She bent over slightly to get the premium book from the coffee table. When she brought her head up, Evan was suddenly standing close enough to kiss her.

Uneasy in her own living room, she leaned backwards as far as she could, then handed him the book. Before taking it and still holding her gaze, he placed his hand over hers momentarily. Helena immediately withdrew her hand and gave him a disapproving look.

"Thank you," he replied in a soft voice as he took the book and scribbled in it.

Helena swallowed hard, snatched the book from Evan, and directed him to the door. "Thank you, Mr. Monahan. Good day," she said with finality. *Now get the hell out of my house! What have I done?* she wondered, slowly shaking her head.

"See you in July," he said, putting on his hat, and in one swell swoop, he was gone.

After getting into his car, Evan paused for a few seconds before putting the key in the ignition. *I touched her. It felt like silk.*

Chapter Nine

Russell knocked on the door, softly at first, and then pounded on it with his fist. All the while, his head darted from left to right to make sure nobody passing on the street could see him standing in the alley. Finally, a gruff voice sounded beyond the door. "What is it and who you know?"

"Russell. Russell Sinclair," he said barely above a whisper. "Nipper invited me."

"Cat got your tongue, nigger?" the voice asked. "I ain't heard nothin' you said."

"Yes you did! Don't play with me, Scottie. Open this damn door, before I kick it in."

Scottie opened the door slowly. "What? You think you the man now? You lucky I like you or your ass would still be standing in the alley," Scottie, the gapped-toothed, muscle-bound, washed-up, punch drunk amateur boxer said as he let Russell in.

"Yeah, yeah," Russell mimicked. Stepping into the dark room, he was assailed by thick cigarette smoke that choked him. Coughing, he asked, "What's hot tonight?"

"Whatever you want—poker, blackjack, craps— and even them fine mommas in the back room."

"That ain't me. Cards, man, just cards," Russell replied as Scottie led him through the maze of smoke to a table where three men were about to start a poker game. Russell paused momentarily and nodded to Nipper who was standing in a corner keeping watch over the activities in the room. Eyeing the men at the table, Russell grabbed the back of one of the vacant chairs at the card table, tipped it backwards, threw his leg over it, and sat down. "Gentlemen, cut me in."

Russell was convinced he'd win big tonight. Plus, he just needed to get out of the house. It was movie night, but Helena insisted they couldn't afford it. Her harping on how little money they had stripped away his confidence. Until now, he felt good about their life. Then there was her fear of getting pregnant too soon after her last miscarriage. It really put a damper on their relationship. Of late, the spontaneity was gone, and it only served to make him feel more inadequate. He'd show Helena tonight.

♣

Helena took a final look at herself in the mirror by the steps. To her delight, the dark circles beneath her eyes were finally gone and she felt good. She picked up her purse and headed out the front door. She walked a block to Fulton Avenue, turned left, and went a block to the house Natalie shared with an aunt. Instead of walking up the three steps to the door, Helena stood on tiptoes and rang the bell.

Shortly after she punched the button, she heard an upstairs window being raised. In anticipation of Natalie's usual response, Helena stepped away from the house and looked up.

"Be down in a sec," Natalie called, poking her head out of the window.

"If only that were true," Helena responded, laughing as her friend retreated and slammed the window down. Helena adjusted her coral sheath dress and sat on the steps to wait. Her thoughts turned to Russell. He had left the house in a huff—to go for a drink with the fellas she guessed. She didn't like refusing him his 'due diligence' any more than he liked being refused, but the timing had to be right if she didn't want to get pregnant too soon after her last miscarriage.

Her thoughts were interrupted when Natalie bounced out the house in a blue and purple paisley shirtwaist dress. "Where to? But first, to what do I owe the pleasure of your company on your movie night?!" she said with her hands on her hips.

"Nothing. I just didn't feel like going."

"Yeah, right! You'd rather go out with me instead of your husband! I don't think so. I may have just gotten off the boat, but I wasn't born on the boat! What gives?"

"Nothing really. Nothing that won't work itself out. We're just a little out of sync since the miscarriage."

"Hmmm—translated—you ain't givin' the boy none!" Natalie laughed.

"It's not funny Natalie. It's not funny!"

"I know. I mean, as much as I can know, especially since I don't have a husband. Helena, sometimes you have to laugh to keep from crying. It'll work out. You and Russell are meant for each other. You know there are other things you can do—" Natalie began, until Helena clamped her hands over her mouth.

"Shut up! I know! Just shut up and come on," Helena said angrily, getting up from the steps and brushing herself off.

"Umm, sensitive, aren't we? Where to?" Natalie responded, shaking her car keys.

"The Avenue, New Haven Lounge."

"Yes ma'am. But, I don't know if I want to go with you. I need to hang out with my single friends because, even though you're a man-magnet, the minute you turn 'em down, they leave."

"They approach me because I'm safe—wedding ring and all. But you, you look desperate. You need to chill."

"Now it's your turn to shut up!"

They walked to the curb, got in Natalie's car, and headed for Pennsylvania Avenue.

Chapter Ten

The poker game ended badly but predictably, with Russell losing. He pushed himself away from the table, and then pulled himself up to his full height. He stumbled toward the door, shrugging off Scottie's attempt to guide him to the exit.

"Look man," Scottie said, trying to steady Russell. "I know you ain't got no money, but one of them fools out there don't know that. They'll hit you in the head thinkin' you do, and beat the shit outta you when they find out you don't. Let me get you a cab. You can't walk home in your condition."

Still trying to avoid Scottie's grasp, Russell weaved toward the door. "What condition?" My wife has a condition. I don't have a condition!" he slurred.

Ignoring the ramblings of a drunk, Scottie grabbed Russell by the arm, walked him up the alley, and shoved him into the taxicab waiting at the curb. He handed the driver several bills.

"Take him to his house on Walbrook Avenue and make sure he gets in."

"You got it. And thank Mr. Nipper for me," the cabbie said, nodding in the direction of a silhouette standing in the middle of the alley.

The cab made its way the short distance to Russell's house. "Hey you," the cabbie yelled. "Here we are. You're home. Can you make it?"

"Yeah," Russell said, opening the door. "Thanks."

Russell wasn't nearly as inebriated as he pretended to be. He thought if he acted drunk, his gambling partners would let their guard down, and he could catch them cheating. He was convinced they were. How else could he have lost so much money? His entire pay check, plus fifty dollars that went on the books. Nipper may not have taken his I.O.U. had he been sober. An argument would have ensued, and there would have been fisticuffs. The bouncers would have made sure Nipper got the upper hand in that situation, but there was no glory in beating a drunken man to a bloody pulp.

Russell fumbled for his door keys and let himself in. *Russell, old man, you better get your stuff together. You can't keep doing this. What's Helena going to say? Nothing! She can't say nothing! I ain't talking to her anyway. What did she do to you?* another voice in his head asked. *Nothing! That's the problem, nothing. I'm going to wake her up and make her do something!* The liquor and the guilt kept him company as he climbed the stairs.

"Helena, wake up," Russell said, as he lost his balance and flopped down on the foot of the bed.

"I'm not sleep. What do you want Russell?"

"So you waited up for me? You know what I want."

"No, I wasn't waiting up for you. I just got in."

"What? What you mean, 'you just got in?'" he said, annoyed and thick tongued. "It's two o'clock in the morning!"

"Three o'clock. It's three o'clock."

"Three o'clock? That's worse. Ain't no decent woman out 'til three in the morning."

"You were out 'til three, weren't you?"

More irritated, he managed to get himself up and walk to Helena's side of the bed. "I'm a man, you can't do what I do."

"Yeah, right. You're drunk, Russell."

"Nope, not drunk. Just feeling no pain. Well, some pain, but not drunk pain."

"Get in the bed Russell. Better yet, go get in the bed in the back room."

"Right," he said, and saluted Helena. "See you tomorrow. Goodbye!" Fully clothed, he walked around to his side of the bed and laid down. Before long, he was snoring loudly. Helena slipped out of bed and went down the hall.

♣

Russell thought he was dreaming. This dream was a lot more pleasant than the ones he had most of the night. But Helena was actually standing next to the bed pushing something toward him.

"Here, Russell. Take these Anacin tablets. I know you have a hang-over."

"Why would I have—" he started, but realized the futility of denying the obvious, besides, his head was pounding. "Thanks, baby. You're too good to me," he said, popping the pills into his mouth and gulping the water.

"I know, but I'm hooked. I ran a bath for you, so get up."

"Get up? I can't go to church this morning."

"It's Saturday, Russell. No church, but you will get up and get in the tub. There's a cup of coffee and a piece of toast in the bathroom waiting for you." Then she let the top of her baby doll pajamas slip off her shoulders. "We're safe now, so go. I'll be waiting here for you."

Except for his shoes, which Helena had taken off during the night, Russell was still fully clothed. "You let me sleep in my clothes?" he said, slowly getting up from the bed.

"Hush, Russell. Don't push your luck. Go on down the hall."

He opened his mouth to respond but thought better of it. He realized he was indeed a lucky man and he needed to enjoy the moment because his wife's good will was destined to run out.

Chapter Eleven

The July heat forced Helena to cook dinner—meatloaf, string beans, and biscuits—early in the morning so the house would be cool at dinnertime. The potatoes, which wouldn't take long and generate much heat, were peeled and diced and sitting in cold water, to be cooked just before Russell got home.

She was happy. She didn't even mind that it was the first Monday of the month. She and the love of her life were back on the same wavelength. Russell, who had shunned having to use condoms as a reward bestowed on people who were married, finally agreed to use them on days when she was "not safe." The rhythm method was no fun, and she prayed her calculations were correct, but they were adjusting.

She would have been less happy, angry in fact, had she known Russell was borrowing money—a little here, a little there—from his friends to pay his latest gambling debts.

Hearing the doorbell peal, she covered her biscuits with a tea-towel, and headed for the door. *It must be Evan,* she thought sarcastically as she proudly pulled out the server drawer to retrieve the insurance book and the July premium.

Exuberantly flinging open the front door, she suddenly froze in place. It was not Evan at all, but a squatty, balding, red-faced man in a cheap searsucker suit, sweating profusely. Regaining her composure, Helena sized-up the man. "Whatever you're selling, I don't want any. Excuse me. Good day." Shooing the man away, she peered around him to see if *Evan* was pulling up. Seeing no sign of him, she started to close the door.

"Mrs. Sinclair, is it?" the man asked hesitantly. "I'm Wilson Chumley, from Beneficial Life," he replied in a halting voice. Before he continued, he pulled a white handkerchief with a red and blue plaid border from his back pocket, and wiped the perspiration from his forehead. "I have a letter from the main office. They usually mail these things– certified," he said more to himself than to Helena, as he reached into his jacket pocket.

"A letter?" Helena questioned. "Where is Mr. Monahan?"

"Who? Mrs.—um—Mrs.—yes, Sinclair?" he replied after looking at the name on the letter again.

"Mr. Monahan," she responded emphatically. "My agent."

"Monahan. Monahan," he mumbled. "Don't know that name. Then it's a big company. I don't know all the route salesmen. Actually, I don't know any route salesmen. At least, not this route."

"You have to know him. He is one of your leading salesmen."

"Well, maybe yes. Monahan, you say. The name is vaguely familiar, but I don't get involved in such things. I'm just a lowly clerk. Why they sent me, I don't know. Anyway, yes. As I said, I have this letter for you. The main office said your route, uh, agent, had an emergency, and they, uh, sent me, Wilson Chumley. A letter usually means your insurance, uh, your insurance, uh, has lapsed."

"Impossible! You don't know what you're talking about Wilson Chumley. Impossible! My insurance is paid up. Here's my book." She shoved it in his face. "See for yourself." If it were not for her concern for her own situation, she would have called an ambulance for Wilson Chumley who looked as if he were having a heart attack.

Wiping the back of his neck this time, Wilson took the book. "See here, miss. There's no entry for May and June. See. Look," he said, pointing to the spot in the book where she assumed Evan had signed off.

Baffled and shocked, she stood there mouth open, wide-eyed, and unable to speak for a moment. When she did, it was in a whisper. "I don't understand. There must be a mistake—"

"Could be, but I doubt it," was Wilson's officious reply. "The company does not make mistakes. Here's my card. Well, a company card. You can call the number on there and somebody will help you. Maybe reinstate you. I don't know."

"Can I get Mr. Monahan on this number?"

"I don't know. Not familiar with that name. That's the main office. You can call—sorry. I have to go. Good day, Miss." With that, he handed the book back to Helena, wiped his forehead again, and headed down the steps.

Helena was sure she would faint. In what seemed like slow motion, she closed the front door, walked to the living room and collapsed on the sofa. *How could this be? Why didn't I look at the book? Why did Evan pretend to make an entry?*

She stared blankly at the business card Wilson Chumley had given her for several minutes before she got up and went to the dining room. Woodenly, she picked up the phone and dialed the number on the card. The phone rang, and rang, and rang, but nobody answered. Clasping her hand on her mouth, she leaned on the wall for support.

With beads of perspiration forming on her forehead, she fished for the Yellow Pages from the bottom of the china closet. "Insurance companies, insurance companies," she said, flipping through the pages. Finding the section, her finger skimmed the list, but she did not find 'North American Beneficial Life and Casualty Insurance Company.' Then she remembered the letter she had angrily dropped on the living room floor. She tore at the envelope and read it. The letter head had a New York City—New York City—telephone number. Calling it would mean a long distance phone charge, but she had no choice. Her heart in her throat, Helena dialed the operator and gave her the phone number. Not knowing what to expect, Helena held her breath as the phone rang. To her surprise and delight, a crisp professional voice answered after only two rings. "North American Beneficial Life and Casualty Insurance Company. May I help you?"

"Yes, I hope so," a nervous Helena replied. "May I speak to Mr. Monahan."

"And you are?"

"Me? I'm one of his—customers, uh, clients."

"May I have your policy number please?"

"May I just speak with Mr. Monahan?" Helena responded, a little irritated.

"I need your policy number, Miss. Miss—?"

"Mrs. Sinclair. My policy number is S47982."

"Thank you, Mrs. Sinclair. I'll have a clerk pull your records and someone will get back to you."

"I need to speak to someone now! Is Mr. Monahan there?"

"I'm afraid no Mr. Monahan works in this office. This is corporate headquarters. I believe he is in the Mid-Atlantic Region. Hold please." And the voice left the phone. After what seemed like an eternity, the voice returned. "Mrs. St. Claire—"

"Sinclair, Sinclair."

"Yes, sorry, Sinclair. Mrs. Sinclair, according to personnel, a Mr. E. Monahan is on vacation for the next two weeks. Can someone else help you?"

"No! No, they cannot. I need to speak—"

The voice cut her off. "Leave your number and I will see that Mr. E. Monahan calls you when he returns."

Furious, Helena barked her number and slammed the phone down. Again, she asked herself the question, *"What have I done?"* She paced back and forth in the dining room, contemplating what she should do next. Suddenly, it occurred to her that there should be a number on the back of the premium book. Violá—a toll free number. She dialed the number and somebody picked up.

"North American Casualty and Life. May I help you?"

"Excuse me. I thought I was calling Beneficial Life Insurance."

"Yes ma'am. We serve them as well. Is this a new claim or a status update?"

"No, neither. I'd like to speak to someone about my policy."

"Is this a new claim?"

"No, it's not a claim," Helena announced emphatically.

"This is the Claims Department and we only handle claims," came the insistent voice. "Your route salesman can handle all other concerns."

A frustrated Helen raised her voice, "That's just the problem! I can't get a hold of him!"

"I'm sorry, Miss, but I can't help you." Then the woman hung up.

A very exasperated Helena contemplated calling Natalie or even Clarice, who she thought would have some knowledge of these kinds of things.

Even though Mose and Russell were good friends and hung out together, Helena and Clarice had limited contact. Helena liked Clarice well enough but considered her an older woman with whom she had little in common. She decided to give the idea of reaching out to Clarice some more thought because she did not want to reveal how stupid she had been.

In the meantime, her head was throbbing. She went upstairs to the medicine cabinet for two Anacin tablets and a cold rag for her forehead. After she downed the pills, she crawled into bed.

♣

Like clockwork, Russell turned the key in the door at four-thirty. "Hey, Helena!" he yelled. "It's me." Getting no response, he headed for the basement per his usual ritual, but found no lights on there and his wife missing. "Hey, Helena! You upstairs?"

Helena squirmed and put her hands over her ears.

Changed into the everyday clothes he kept in the basement, Russell bounded up the two flights of stairs to find Helena in bed. "Wondered why you didn't answer me," he said, concerned as he walked over to the bed and sat on the edge. "What's the matter? Don't feel good? Are you sick?"

"Just a headache. Can you heat up your own dinner?"

"Yeah, sure, but what gave you the headache?"

"What gave me the headache? Headaches just happen, Russell. Could you just go fix your dinner?"

"Yep. Sorry you don't feel well," he said, as he kissed her on the forehead. Tiptoeing out of the room, he headed downstairs. Once in the kitchen, he turned the burner on low under the string beans, then sliced two pieces of meatloaf and put them in the frying pan with the gravy. Cold biscuits were okay, but what was he supposed to do with raw white potatoes in a bowl of cold water?

Chapter Twelve

Feet resting on a leather hassock, Chaz tapped the end of a Lucky Strike on his silver-plated cigarette case. As he lit it, he watched Evan pour a drink from the crystal flask that was on the hostess cart. Evan always teased him that the wood, glass, and leather décor scattered throughout the apartment needed a feminine touch, but Chaz was perfectly content with it.

With bourbon in hand, Evan flopped down on the matching leather sofa. "I'll call Rebecca myself, but be sure to thank her for me when you talk to her."

"You know my cousin is so infatuated with you, she'll do anything for you—without even asking questions. Not me! I want to know what you're up to," Chaz said good naturedly.

"Up to? Nothing."

"You're lucky Rebecca had a lay-over in Manhattan this week or this little game you're playing—whatever it is—wouldn't have worked. What gives?"

"Just having a little fun with a friend. A practical joke," Evan said, as he sipped his drink.

"Practical joke? A friend? Rebecca said the woman sounded distraught *and* she said the woman sounded colored!"

"Look, I asked you for a favor. Like a good friend, you complied. I appreciate it. That's all you need to know. The woman wasn't colored—but so what if she was."

"I dunno. Nothing I guess," Chaz responded a little defensively. "Rebecca was worried the woman would go off script and she wouldn't know what to say. Come on, Evan, what are you up to?"

"I told you, nothing, a practical joke. It's done!" Evan said, clearly irritated. He got up to pour himself another drink. With his back to Chaz, he smiled.

♣

He didn't know how or why he had hatched this plan, but he was fully committed to it. He believed it would get him to his ultimate goal. Chumley had been easy. As a clerk in the regional office, he did what he was told. Evan had simply gotten the office secretary to assign Chumley the task of delivering the letter, the contents of which neither was aware. All the secretary knew—or thought she knew—was the order had come from corporate. Evan had gotten the phony business card printed and the letter typed on his own. He had been fairly certain Helena would not look up the company in the phone book, but on the off chance she did, he knew she'd never find it. The North American Beneficial Life and Casualty Insurance Company was a wholly owned subsidiary of the Monahan Investment Group, Ltd, and was not listed independently in the Yellow Pages. This relationship was on Beneficial Life's real business cards.

Rebecca had been easy, too. As a stewardess with New York as her home base, she shared an apartment in Manhattan with a co-worker. Generally, she had a one-week layover at home every six weeks. It was her phone number on the infamous letter Chumley had given to Helena.

To make sure everything went smoothly, Evan had given Rebecca a script with optional responses, depending on Helena's questions. Rebecca always thought Evan was a 'hoot' and, wanting to please him, went along with what she thought was a joke.

Returning to the sofa with his second drink, Evan was met by an intense stare from his friend, which momentarily disarmed him. He felt his stomach churning as he sat down.

"I hope to hell you know what you're doing," Chaz said, taking a drag of his cigarette.

"Of course I do," Evan responded, with more confidence than he felt.

Chapter Thirteen

Helena took off the one-size too big pea green uniform and hung it on the hook in her locker. As it turned out, Russell had to eat his words—his wife went to work. Helena landed a job as an elevator operator at Stewart's Department Store on the northeast corner of Howard and Lexington Streets where she worked part-time from 10:00 a.m. to 3:00 p.m., Tuesday through Friday.

She was grateful for the job but hated the uniform. The company could care less about the fit of the operators' regulation clothing as long as the ladies were polite, smiled, got the customer to the right floor, and was as inconspicuous as possible.

When she took the job almost a month ago, she anticipated having discretionary money to not only buy a washing machine, but to occasionally buy some of the beautiful clothes in Stewart's. It didn't matter to her that colored customers were relegated to shop in the basement and were not allowed to try on the clothing before buying them. It was a fact of the times, which she accepted.

Before taking the job, she could not have imagined how empowering earning her own money could be. But, unfortunately, her discretionary money had become money to cover shortages brought on by Russell's continued gambling. If anybody had told her Russell would become irresponsible with his money, she would have told them they were crazy. For the life of her, she could not figure out when he changed. Lately, it had become a major bone of contention between them. The job got her out of the house and took her mind off finances and the Beneficial Life dilemma.

Helena changed into a straight skirt and ruffled blouse and buckled a cinch belt around her narrow waist. After applying some lipstick, she closed her locker, turned the dial on the combination lock, and left the store.

During the bus trip home, she relaxed and turned over in her mind how she was going to present her ultimatum to Russell. When she turned the key in the door, she was startled to find Russell sitting on the sofa with an ice bag on his left hand.

"Russell, you scared me. You're a little early. What happened to your hand?"

"Hey, baby. Hurt it at work. I hit it with a hammer. Nothing broken, though," he replied.

Looking at him skeptically, Helena walked over to the sofa, sat down, and put one arm around his shoulder. With her other hand, she examined Russell's hand as he winced. "Wow, it's pretty swollen, but what are those marks?"

"I guess the claw got me."

"The claw? A three-claw hammer? What kind of hammering were you doing to hit yourself with the claw side? Looks like you would have broken some bones to leave those kinds of marks. Why don't I believe you?" Helena said, as she rotated Russell's hand.

"Ouch, Helena. Stop!" Russell yelped, snatching his hand from her grasp. "Okay. I wasn't paying attention to what I was doing. I was too busy arguing about last night's Orioles' game."

"You were doing what? You got that distracted over baseball to do damage to yourself?"

"Yeah. We had a minor difference of opinion," he said, trying to laugh.

"You gotta be kidding me. I don't believe one bit of it!"

"I don't know why not."

"For Pete's sake, Russell!" Helena said, standing up. With one hand on her hip, and a finger pointed in her husband's face, she shouted, "You keep screwing up and you're going to lose not only your job, but all you've worked for and ME!"

Russell reached for her with his good hand. "Wait a minute, baby. I think you're overreacting."

"Think so? Baseball my ass! You know you're lying."

♣

In fact, he was. Russell had just left the portable toilet and was heading for the makeshift lunch area the workers had carved out at the edge of the construction site when Pee Wee—one of Nipper's henchmen—jumped him. Two inches taller than the five-foot eleven assailant, Russell easily catapulted Pee Wee over his shoulder.

Russell's 180 pounds—twenty fewer than Pee Wee's—was ripped with muscles developed from working a few stints with a jackhammer and gave him a decided advantage.

Pee Wee landed on his rear end and grinned at Russell as he scrambled to his feet.

"Sinclair. You're two weeks behind, and I came to collect."

"You and whose army? Does Nipper know you're sittin' down on the job? Get out of here, Pee Wee. I told Nipper to keep you clowns away from my job."

"You ain't in no position to threaten nobody. Pay up or else." Pee Wee reached in his pocket and the sunlight bounced off the blade of his knife as it clicked open. He lounged at Russell, slicing a two-inch gash in his shirt.

As Russell sucked in his midsection, Pee Wee swung again, but missed his target. Then, in rapid succession, Russell delivered two right hooks which landed squarely in the would-be-assailant's mouth.

Pee Wee spit out blood and teeth as several men approached to break up the confrontation. One of whom was Russell's foreman who sent Russell home, suspended for the rest of the week.

Chapter Fourteen

It was Monday, and Helena was off, two-weeks to the day of Wilson Chumley's visit. More calls to the New York telephone number had gone unanswered. She paced the length of the downstairs in anticipation of hearing from Evan Monahan, not knowing if he would call or come by. When the doorbell peeled, she was startled. Collecting herself, she went to the door and opened it slowly.

For a few seconds, she and Evan stood staring at each other, and then both started to speak at the same time. Both stopped, waited a second, and started again. Though there was tension in the air, neither could help smiling.

Evan nodded. "You first."

"Mr. Monahan, you have a lot of explaining to do."

"Yes, ma'am. May I come in?" a falsely contrite Evan asked.

Helena stepped aside, and Evan walked into the living room and made himself comfortable as had become his habit. Helena ignored it.

"Explain Wilson Chumley to me," Helena demanded, standing over Evan with her hands on her hips.

"Please sit, Mrs. Sinclair," Evan said, patting the space next to him.

"Don't you dare ask me to sit in my own house! Why has my insurance lapsed? Why didn't you apply my loan to the premium?" she demanded.

"I'm sorry, but please sit. There's been a terrible mistake." Evan spoke softly, taking the wind out of Helena's sail. She relented and sat down, then angled toward Evan so she could look him straight in the eyes.

"Let's see," Evan began, taking out a notebook. "At this point, you're insurance hasn't been paid in three months."

"What do you mean—three months?" You said you'd lend me the money. You have my I.O.U., Mr. Monahan."

"You know, Mrs. Sinclair," he said with a half-smile. "I've been coming here for over a year. We ought to be on a first name basis by now, don't you think?"

81

Caught off guard, Helena stumbled over her words. "I don't know about that, Mr. Monahan. Ours is a business relationship. I don't know anything about you personally, and you don't know anything about me."

"Guess you're right, but I do know a little something about you. I know you've been married for four years. I know you and Russell are both twenty-three years old, and I know you're one of the prettiest colored girls I've ever seen. I also know Russell has a heart murmur, but I managed to get him insurance anyway," he said smugly.

Taken aback, Helena's heart raced. "What are you driving at, Mr. Monahan?"

"Evan. Call me Evan. Driving at? Why nothing. Just making small talk. Didn't mean to offend," he said, handing the book back to Helena. "But, maybe there is something you could do about your delinquent payments." He leaned forward in an attempt to kiss her on the neck.

Without a second thought, Helena slapped him and stood up. "Have you lost your mind, Mr. Monahan? You need to leave. If I tell my husband about this—"

"Your husband? The gambler who hangs out with dangerous men, and who has a heart murmur and really doesn't qualify for insurance. That husband?"

"Get out before I call the police."

"Calm down," Evan responded. "I'll be gone before they get here, and besides, what will you say to them? And do you think they'll believe what you tell them?"

"What do you want?" As soon as the words came out of her mouth, Helena knew that was the wrong question. She started for the door, but Evan grabbed her and pulled her back on the sofa. Pinning her down with an arm across her chest, he began to slide one hand up her thigh.

"Get off of me! Get off!" Helena yelled, as she tried to free herself.

"Please don't fight me. You know I won't hurt you," Evan answered calmly as he shifted his weight. "You can easily bring your book up to date for the rest of the year."

His expensive cologne assaulted her nose. "Get the hell off me!" she hissed, still trying to push him off, but he was surprisingly strong and rock solid. With her left arm pinned beneath her, she flailed her right arm and managed to scratch his face. Evan grabbed her arm, but she continued to struggle.

"Please, Helena, stop. I won't hurt you."

She attempted to kick him, but she was in an awkward position and the move proved unwise. Evan shifted his entire body weight on top of her, then managed to lift her dress and spread her legs with his free hand.

"Stop, Helena. I love you," he whispered as he fumbled with her underwear.

He loves me? Oh, please God. Don't let this happen. She was so shocked by Evan's words that, for a split second, all the fight went out of her. Though he was clumsy, it was just enough time for him to get the upper hand and enter her. She struggled under his weight and pummeled his back. To no avail. Within a minute, he moaned, exploded inside her and went limp atop her.

"No! No! Oh, God No!" Helena cried. She reached over her head to the table next to the sofa, fumbling for anything she could use as a weapon. In the process, she sent a lamp crashing to the floor, but managed to pick up a square glass ashtray with pointed corners. She smashed it against Evan's head.

Mortified but oblivious to the pain and the blood trickling down his forehead, Evan quickly rolled off Helena and dropped to the floor. He seemed dazed and confused as he nervously pulled up his trousers.

"I'm sorry, so sorry—" he said, as he fumbled with his clothing, then ran out the front door, leaving a distraught Helena crying and screaming.

"Get out! Get out you bastard and never come back!" she yelled after the fleeing Evan.

That was not the way it was supposed to happen. Evan had rehearsed it over and over in his mind. In his fantasy, she willingly gave herself to him. This was not supposed to happen; he was devastated. How could he have done this terrible thing, and how could he have lost control so easily? He had planned to carefully and fully indulge in her womanhood. Have her passion match his. Instead, it was over in a humiliating second—before he could bask in the silky caramel skin, or kiss the sensual full lips, or feast on forbidden fruit, or hear her moan his name. Now he could never show his face in her house again.

Driving aimlessly at breakneck speed through residential neighborhoods, Evan pulled the car over, opened the door, and threw up.

With gut-retching sobs and hot fury, Helena yanked the chair cover from the sofa and dragged it to the foot of the stairs, where she dropped it. Trance-like, she climbed the stairs and went into the bathroom to rid herself of Evan's disgusting essence. She was barely conscious of what she was doing as she sank into the tub and scrubbed herself with a vengeance—punishing herself for something over which she had no control. Hardly aware of the passage of time, she emerged from the tub, only after the water became cold. With tears streaming down her cheeks, she made her way to the bedroom and mechanically dressed herself. Then she made it downstairs to put the slipcover into a laundry basket. She didn't know whether to throw it away or take it to the Laundromat. Discarding it would mean making up something to tell Russell. She thought about rearranging the living room furniture, as if that would somehow erase what happened.

As she tried in vain to move the sofa, the telephone rang. She shrank from the sound as if the instrument was a hissing cobra, ready to attack. Reluctantly, she went to the dining room to answer it.

"Hello," she said in a barely audible whisper.

"Helena? Helena?" came the voice. "What's the matter? Did you hear already?"

Confused, she repeated the greeting. "Hello. Who is this? Hear what?"

"Helena, this is Mose. Did the hospital call you already?"

"Mose? Hospital? Just a minute, please," she said, as she put the phone down, pulled out a chair, and sat down. She was feeling lightheaded and needed a minute to collect herself. A little panicked, she steeled herself and picked up the phone. "Now tell me slowly, Mose. I didn't get a call—is Russ—?"

Before she could finish, Mose interrupted her. "I'm sorry to come at you like that, but you sounded upset already, so I thought you had heard somehow. Nothing serious–too serious—anyway. Russell will be just fine, but the hand he hurt a few days ago, needs tending to. Doctor says it's infected real bad. We're at Provident. Can you get a ride, catch a cab or something, and come?"

"Of course. Yes. Are you telling me the truth, Mose? Is he really all right?"

"Yeah, he's all right. I wouldn't lie to you about a thing like that. But are you all right? You sound funny. You sounded strange when you picked up."

"Guess you caught me dozing and the phone startled me. Let me go so I can get to the hospital.

Thanks Mose. Talk to you later." For the moment, her horrific experience was pushed to the back of her mind so she could deal with her current crises. She realized she should have asked Mose more about how Russell had hurt his hand because she was convinced his previous version was not the truth.

♣

When Helena got to the ER, she was surprised and relieved to find Russell pacing in the waiting room. An agitated Mose, was shaking his head while he watched him from beside a water fountain.

Immediately, Helena rushed to Russell and embraced him. "Russell, are you all right? I know it's not his fault, but Mose scared me to death."

"I'm kinda all right. They want to keep me here. They say my hand is badly infected, and if I don't stay and get it treated, I could lose it!"

"What!" a shocked Helena said. "How could it get that infected? You've been soaking it in Epsom salt and stuff."

Mose joined the two of them. "You know a human mouth is filthy. A human bite is the worse kinda bite you can get, especially from a Nipper thug," he said with a nod.

Helena looked straight into Russell's eyes, but spoke to Mose. "What are you talking about?" she asked slowly.

"Aw, shit," Mose said, putting his hand over mouth. "Guess I stepped in it."

"Somebody had better tell me something before I get loud in here!" Helena said through clenched teeth.

"Let's sit down," Russell said, as he pulled Helena toward a chair. "I didn't hit it with a hammer. I got into a fight. Went I hit the joker in the mouth, his teeth went into my hand. Those were the marks you saw. Now it's infected and needs immediate attention, or they may have to amputate it."

Speechless, Helena got up from the sofa and walked away. She ducked into the first ladies room she came to. Once inside, she leaned against the wall and pounded it with both fists. *What else Lord? What else?* The incident with Russell would have been less devastating, had she not been so fragile already.

When she emerged from the bathroom red-eyed, Mose was waiting for her. He took her hand and they walked down the hall. "He let them admit him. I'll take you to his room. I know it's easier said than done, but don't worry. He'll be all right. I think he's learned his lesson. The boss said if there's another—"

Helena stopped in her tracks. "Another? What do you mean 'another?'"

"Uh, poor choice of words. I guess 'any other' is better. Any other incidents and Russell's gone. Russell's a good man; he just made a mistake. He said you threatened to leave him."

"That wasn't a threat," she said out loud, but the heaviness in the pit of her stomach told her she might have to leave for reasons she would never have imagined.

Mose left her at the elevator with instructions to call if she needed a ride home. When she reached Russell's room, the attending physician was leaving and a nurse was hooking Russell up to an IV with a penicillin drip.

"Are you Mrs. Sinclair?" the doctor asked, from the doorway of Russell's room. When Helena nodded silently, he explained Russell's condition. "Your husband has a very serious infection and needs to be on an intravenous antibiotic for the next seven to ten days. It's going to be very painful because every day the surgeon will have to scrape out any new tissue that grows to be sure there are no bacteria in the wound. He'll do that until he's sure all the infection is gone. The good news is, he won't lose the hand now that he's in the hospital. Any questions?"

"No. Thank you, doctor," Helena said with downcast eyes, and then went into the room.

She was not going to argue with Russell. All the fight was gone. Evan had proven she was in control of nothing. Instead, she just walked over to the bed and kissed her husband. Then the sobs came.

Russell felt powerless to do anything but listen to his wife cry. He had no idea she would be so affected by his mishap. He loved his wife too much to hurt her so deeply. He vowed to clean up his act.

Chapter Fifteen

Finally pulling himself together, Evan drove home on auto-pilot. He had no idea how he got there, but he parked and let himself in. He stood in the foyer for a minute, trying to figure out what was wrong—besides what had already occurred. Something felt out of place, but he couldn't fathom what. Then suddenly it came to him. *No Lena. Where is Lena?* The Abyssinian did not greet him or come when he called. Hoping his mother had an answer, he hurried to the sunroom, but his mother was not there. He walked through the patio door and found her weeding her flower bed. "Mother, have you seen Lena? She didn't meet me at the door. Where is she?"

"Good afternoon to you, too," his mother responded without looking up. "Lena's missing in action, but I'm sure she'll return. Ressy looked for her this afternoon, but no sign."

Evan tried not to sound overwrought, though the irony did not escape him. "Sorry Mother. Hello. It's not like Lena to run away. I need to go look for her," he said, as he started for the gate.

Maureen Monahan finally looked up at her son. "Good God, Evan! What happened to you? You're disheveled and you smell of vomit. Is that blood over your eye?"

Evan kept walking toward the end of the yard. "Nothing happened to me," he insisted. *Nothing and everything.* He felt himself on the verge of tears as he opened the gate.

"Get back here, Evan! This minute! You will not leave this yard looking like that. What is wrong with you? What happened to you?" his mother insisted.

Evan paused for a minute with his hand on the gate but closed it slowly and walked back to the house, avoiding his mother's questioning gaze. When he went back through the sunroom, Ressy, his mother's housekeeper and companion, met him in the hallway holding Lena whose silky coat was matted and dirty.

"Mr. Evan, I just found Lena. I guess she was looking for a little excitement," Ressy laughed. The dictates of her subservient roll required she call Evan 'Mister' even though he was just five years older.

Evan reached for the cat and both he and Ressy were shocked when she snarled and tried to scratch him. "Lena, it's me. What's gotten into you, girl?" Evan said reaching for her again. "Nice kitty. Nice kitty. Come to daddy."

"Never saw her do that," Ressy said, forcing the cat into Evan's waiting hands. Ressy hated cats, but tolerated Lena. After all, she had to. She worked there.

♣

Reesy had worked for the Monahans in one role or another since she was fourteen. Her grandmother had worked for the family when they lived in South Carolina, and as a teenager, Ressy spent the summers helping her grandmother. Many times during those summers, Evan teased, joked and played with Ressy, though as an adult, he didn't acknowledge it. His father, Connor III, stringently objected to the relationship, proclaiming Evan was too familiar with the help.

Even though Ressy performed menial tasks, she had loved the Monahan house and had enjoyed sharing her grandmother's room. When she returned to school, she always pretended she had spent her vacation at her family's summer home in South Carolina. Once the Monahan's moved to Baltimore and her grandmother passed away, Ressy automatically took over the job.

Since his fortune had grown, Connor III was rarely at the Roland Park address, and Ressy, thankfully, saw little of him. In fact, his wife saw little of him, but was content with the life he afforded her, especially since her health was declining and she could not be the wife she once was.

♣

When Evan started toward the stairs with Lena in his arms, she scratched him. Startled, he dropped her, and she scampered to the sunroom. "What's wrong with that damn cat?" he said to nobody in particular.

Ressy shook her head. "Don't know, Mr. Evan. Maybe, since she's been out, you need to take her to the vet."

"Yeah, maybe," Evan responded as he dejectedly walked up the steps to his room and slammed the door. He picked up the telephone on his night table and dialed Chaz's number.

After several rings, Chaz picked up. "Hildebrandt. May I help you?"

"Yeah, Chaz. I need to talk to you," Evan said desperately.

"Evan, old man. What are you into now? I'm at work. You know I work for a living."

"Stop with the bullshit, Chaz. Not now. I need to talk to you!"

"Shoot."

"Not over the phone. Can you meet me at O'Doulie's?"

"Not until I finish here. Not until about five-thirty—"

Evan hung up without letting Chaz finish. *Never mind. Bad idea anyway. No need spilling my guts. What's done is done. I just need to get on with it.* He fished a flask out of his desk drawer and poured himself two shots of bourbon. His mother was right. He looked a mess and smelled worse. Once he peeled off his clothes, he threw them toward his waste basket and got in the shower.

Chapter Sixteen

After ten days in the hospital, Russell was finally released and sent home with a fourteen-day regime of antibiotics and instructions not to return to work for a week. On Russell's scheduled release date, Helena went straight to the hospital from work without changing into her street clothes. Natalie was meeting her there to drive them home. Helena was relieved Russell was coming home because she needed her husband there to feel safe. She wanted him close, and she wanted to be in his arms. But she had no idea how she would respond to intimacy, because misplaced guilt and shame were a constant knot in her stomach.

♣

Natalie Grant had left home at thirteen to live with her aunt Loretta when her mother remarried. She hated her stepfather, though her brother got along with him just fine. Loretta had a lovely home on Fulton Avenue and, at nearly forty, chose to remain single. The idea of being "stuck" with one man for her whole life was anathema to her. She preferred variety, which got her both talked about and envied by her peer group. The house was a three-story one, and Natalie occupied the third floor where she had absolute privacy and isolation from her aunt's affairs – figuratively and literally.

Natalie and Helena had been best friends since they met in junior high, and though Natalie hated to admit it to herself, she was sometimes jealous of her friend. In her opinion, Helena had the best husband in the world and a great life. Russell was good looking—not Belafonte good looking—but pleasing to the eye. He was kind and devoted to his wife. She did notice, though, Russell was quite different when he wasn't around Helena. She knew this first hand because she frequented some of the places he did, when he hung out with Mose or some of his other buddies – places neither he nor she would ever take Helena. In those places, Russell was a little louder, a little more course, and flirted with the barmaids. Natalie never saw him do anything that concerned her, but then she always left soon after spotting him to make sure she never did. Her leaving, however, worked both ways. She didn't see him, and he didn't see her.

♣

Lately, Natalie was concerned about Helena. When she had visited her friend during Russell's stay in the hospital, she found the living room in disarray. "What gives?" she had asked Helena.

According to Helena, she had grown tired of the way the furniture was arranged and tried to change it but found the pieces too heavy to move. The two of them managed to get the couch back where it belonged. That story explained the sofa's angle, but not the mismatched chair covers. Then there was the inch of dust she observed everywhere; Helena always dusted. Natalie decided it was a result of the demands of work and hospital visits leaving Helena no time or energy to clean. Yet, Natalia sensed there was something else not attributable to Russell's hospitalization or even the temporary loss of income. When Helena was ready to open up, she'd be there to listen.

♣

Natalie dropped her charges off at the door, waved goodbye and was gone. Like most men, Russell was oblivious to the change of décor in his living room.

"Whew," he said, easing himself onto the sofa. "Ten days in bed sure does zap your strength. I'm bushed. The short trip from the hospital wiped me out."

"I'm just glad to have you home. I missed you," Helena responded.

"Me too. Think I'll wrap this hand in some plastic and get in a hot bath. Want to come watch and see if I do it right?" he smiled.

"I'm sure you'll manage, but I'll be up in a minute." She watched him go up the steps, then the silent tears returned.

Chapter Seventeen

Two months later, September, 1955

Helena sat on the side of the bath tub, chest heaving and trying to catch her breath. After a few minutes, she was back on her knees at the commode, drenched in sweat, violently retching. She could hear Russell's bare feet hurrying down the hall.

"What's the matter?" he asked from the bathroom door. "You throwing up?"

Unable to answer, Helena continued to retch, but managed, with her head down, to wave Russell away. He didn't leave, but he was quiet, helplessly watching his wife be sick. After an awkward silence, Helena got up off her knees and grabbed a face cloth from the towel bar. Wetting it with cold water, she dabbed her face. "Guess it was something I ate."

"We ate the same thing—" a concerned Russell said, trying to remember the food Greg and his wife had served at their impromptu cook-out the night before. "You only ate one hot dog and some slaw."

"Must have been one hot dog too many," Helena said, resuming her position on the tub's edge.

"Need me to stay home? I will—" Russell began.

"No, of course not. Not for a little upset stomach. As soon as it's all out of me, I'll be fine. You should get ready for work. I think I'm finished in the bathroom. I'll go down to the kitchen and get some pink stuff," she said, after rooting through the medicine cabinet and not finding any. "Maybe gargle with salt water, too." She felt Russell's eyes on her back as she headed down the steps. "You better hurry up or you'll miss Mose," she called over her shoulder.

After seeing Russell off, she climbed back in bed feeling much better. Even so, she vowed to call Dr. Hill when she got up. It was fortuitous that it was her day off and she hoped he would see her without an appointment. As soon as the office opened, Helena made her phone call. The receptionist said Dr. Hill would work her in if she didn't mind a long wait. She didn't.

♣

After almost two hours in the waiting room, Dr. Hill examined her and told her to meet him in his private office where he conferred with patients individually. With a big grin, he walked over to Helena and patted her on the shoulder. "I think congratulations are in order. Looks like you're about eight weeks," he said, as he walked around to his desk. "I won't know for sure until we get the lab work completed." He waited, expecting a response from Helena but got none. "Mrs. Sinclair, I had hoped you would have waited a little longer, but we'll take precaution this time," he said cautiously. "Mrs. Sinclair, what is it?"

"It's just that I, we, tried to be so careful—I'm just not ready—"

"Most people aren't ready when it happens, but at least we know. I hate to ask, but did you tell Mr. Sinclair this time?"

"Yes. I mean, no. I wanted to be sure before I got his hopes up. Plus, with this being so close to the last time, and you told us to wait, he'd be a nervous wreck—" Then the tears came.

Dr. Hill shrugged his shoulders and pushed a tissue box toward Helena as he tried to reassure her. "You're a religious woman, Mrs. Sinclair. Look at it this way. It must be God's plan. I'm going to order bed rest for you for—at least the first trimester—and then we'll see from there. That means steps only once a day, no lifting, no housework, and bed rest all day. You can walk around for about 15 minutes, three times a day, around meal times." He tore off a script from his pad. "These are for prenatal vitamins and my secretary will write you a note for work. That's it.

If Mr. Sinclair has any questions, he can call the office. Don't worry. You and the baby will be fine."

The tears continued as Helena sat there, practically in a state of shock. Dr. Hill gave her a questioning look but rose from his chair and walked around his desk, signaling the session was over.

♣

After the examination with Dr. Hill, Helena spent some time in the restroom regaining her composure and praying. She avoided giving voice to her deepest fear but hoped God would hear her heart. Feeling better, she headed for the bus stop with plans to stop at Pantry Pride to pick up something for a quick dinner, but she debated with herself over the efficacy of filling the prescription for the vitamins.

It was a short ride to the supermarket, but long enough for Helena to reassure herself everything would work out just fine, especially since she had a plan. Walking into the store, Helena spotted Clarice in the produce section, sniffing cantaloupes.

"Hey, Clarice," Helena called, attempting to sound normal.

"Hey yourself," Clarice beamed back. Then she said something to the young boy beside her, who nodded and walked away. "Haven't seen you for a while."

Helena failed to hide the look of curiosity on her face as she approached Clarice and kissed her on the cheek. "We need to get together sometime," she said casting a quick look at the boy putting grapes in a bag. His facial features were non-descript, his skin, pale, almost white, and his hair was a wavy reddish brown. On the left side of his face, above his lip was a prominent brownish mole. If Clarice had anything to do with his birth, it was not evident.

As if she were reading Helena's mind, Clarice spoke matter-of-factly. "That's my son, Ray. I don't think you've ever met him, but I'm sure Mose has mentioned him."

"Ray, oh yes. I remember now." Helena lied. "Russell did tell me. He's a big boy. How old is he?" Helena asked, smiling and waving in Ray's direction.

"Thirteen. He's a little shy. He lives with my parents, but he's up for a couple of weeks for a visit," Clarice explained.

"That's nice," Helena said hurriedly. "Good to see you Clarice. I just stopped for a couple of things— got to run." She pecked Clarice on the cheek again and headed for the meat department.

♣

Clarice was startled at Helena's hasty departure. *Maybe*, she thought, *she was embarrassed by her puffy eyes. She's certainly been crying, crying a lot.* Clarice decided to ask Mose what was going on with the Sinclairs. Young husbands didn't always do the right things.

♣

When Helena got home, she quickly put her groceries away and went into the dining room to make a phone call. After a few minutes, she took a deep breath, and dialed Natalie, who answered as if she were anticipating a call.

"Hello," was the breathless answer.

"Natalie, it's me. I gotta ask you a question."

"I'm just fine, Helena. How are you?"

"Skip the niceties. I have a burning question. This young girl at work has got herself in some trouble, if you know what I mean. Do you know somebody who can help her out?"

"I'm just fine," an irritated Natalie replied. "What kind of trouble, and why are you asking me?"

"Come on Natalie. You know what kind of trouble, and you know why I'm asking you."

"What's her name? You never mentioned a young girl at work before—"

"That's because she and I aren't bosom buddies. I guess she's desperate, you know—young, no money, no husband."

"I do, and I feel for her, but I can't help. It's not right, and you know it's not."

"Since when did you get a conscience—" Helena began, before realizing the insensitivity of her words.

"I don't know how you fixed your mouth to say that to me! Since I learned better, that's when." Then Natalie slammed the phone down, leaving Helena's apology to float in dead air.

Helena stared at the receiver in disbelief after Natalie hung up on her. She slowly put the instrument down. *Now I've insulted my best friend, but I don't think she'll think anything of it. Get a grip, Helena. Think. Think.*

In desperation, she dialed another number. A pleasant, soft voice answered on the other end. "Momma," Helena responded. "It's me. How are you and daddy doing?" Helena could hear the smile in her mother's voice and knew she was beckoning her father to the phone. "Momma, don't call daddy. I'll talk to him after I talk to you. Girl talk."

"Why sure, honey," her mother said, the voice now sounded curious. "How are you? How's Russell?"

"Just fine, Momma. Where's daddy?"

"He's standing in the doorway waiting to talk to you."

"Tell him to leave, please."

"What?"

"Momma, please tell him to leave."

Helena could hear her mother speaking to her father. "Emmanuel, could you excuse us a minute. We have to talk girl talk." After a few seconds, Madeline Wilkes returned to the phone. "What is it?" she asked anxiously.

"Is Miss Ophelia still around?"

"Miss Ophelia? Why do you ask? Why do you want to know about Miss Ophelia?"

"There's this young girl at work who's in a bad way, and she needs somebody like Miss Ophelia," Helena began, but was interrupted by her mother.

"We raised you to carry yourself like a Christian woman. Who would dare ask you such a question?!"

"Momma, you don't understand. I could tell she was going through some rough times. I just reached out to her and she confided in me."

"You're right. I don't understand, and I can't believe you even entertained such a notion. No! You of all people who wants a child and can't keep one in her womb. You should be ashamed. I'm going to pray for you and that young girl, whoever she is. And I'll lie to your father about this conversation."

Smarting from her mother's stinging words, Helena tried to apologize. "I'm sorry, Momma. You're right. I'll call you later." She hung-up, chastising herself for having called her mother, and for putting her in a position to lie to her father. What kind of lie it would be, she had no clue. She realized she had made a catastrophic, strategic mistake. How now was she going to break the news to her mother that she was pregnant? Certainly her mother would not see her inquiry about Miss Ophelia and her condition as coincidental.

For several minutes, she sat at the dining room table with her head in her hands. She contemplated calling Natalie again and apologizing but thought it would only serve to make matters worse. Before she realized it, she nodded off.

When she awoke, some twenty minutes later, she was disoriented, but somehow relieved. She remembered having a pleasant, comforting dream, though she was not certain of its meaning.

In the dream, Helena found herself in her green work uniform, on a hill, overlooking a lush green valley, in the center of which was a field of vibrant purple and pink flowers. The pulsating valley was alive and seemed to draw her, but she was afraid to descend. Suddenly, Natalie appeared in a white lab coat to encourage her to answer the valley's call. Just as Natalie started to push her, Helena found herself transported—as if she were on an elevator—to the meadow of flowers.

As she approached the flowers, she found they were not flowers at all, but rather rainbow-colored cherubim, growing out of the soil. While Helena did not see the gardener, she sensed his presence and his desire for her to pick a cherub-flower.

As soon as she did, she was immediately transported out of the valley to the top of the hill again. When she smiled down at the cherub in her arms, she found a bouquet of purple and pink morning glories instead, singing Brahms Lullaby.

Reluctantly, she got up and went to the kitchen to begin dinner. All she knew was she had to tell Russell the "good news." For the life of her, she couldn't remember why she didn't want to tell her husband she was pregnant.

Chapter Eighteen

Mose downed the last of his after-dinner coffee while Clarice cleared the table and wiped off the oilcloth table covering. He enjoyed this part of the day. Work was forgotten. Mose Jr, their four-year old, was down for the evening, and Ray, who was still visiting, was down the block playing with the only two boys in the neighborhood who did not tease or poke fun at him.

Mose worried Ray's grandparents—his in-laws— sheltered the boy too much and he needed toughening up, but that was not his problem.

With the kids out of sight, he and Clarice had a few minutes for themselves. He contentedly sipped his after-dinner coffee while Clarice finished washing the evening dishes. He watched her as he always did.

She was of medium height, dark brown, top-heavy with narrow hips and thin, some would say *skinny legs*, but she had what counted for him. He enjoyed seeing her move around the tiny kitchen.

Coffee finished, Mose handed Clarice his cup. "What did the old biddy do to you today?" he asked Clarice, referring to her employer.

"Nothing really. Today was a good day for her. She's not so bad most days. I'd just rather be cleaning my own house, that's all," Clarice said loading the sink. "I took her to her flower club meeting today."

"What you mean you took her?" Mose asked with a knowing grin on his face.

"Yep, she let me drive the caddy."

Mose laughed out loud. "I told you, you needed to learn how to drive! How did it feel?"

"I was a little nervous at first, but it felt good. I pretended it was my car! I think she's gonna fire her driver."

"If she do, that'll be a raise for you, won't it? Don't let her try to get two-for-one."

"We'll see. Anyhow, I can't do two jobs, you know."

"I know. Won't be like this all the time. I'm working my way up to construction supervisor. When I get it, you can stay home, raise your own baby, and clean your own house!"

"Sounds too good. You know, construction ain't guaranteed" she began wistfully.

"Clarice, don't rain on my parade, please," he chided her, knowing he was a long way from getting a raise.

"Mose," Clarice said, as she pulled out a chair and sat down. "What's Russell talking about these days?"

"What do you mean? Stuff we always talk about. What you gettin' at?"

"Oh, nothing," she began, as Mose put down his cup and leaned toward her, looking her dead in the eye.

"Nothing, my behind. What do you want to know?"

"I was just wondering how they were doing. I saw Helena in the supermarket today, and she didn't look so good."

"That's kind of hard for her to do," he grinned, despite knowing Clarice was put off by his comments on Helena's good looks.

She slapped his hand. "I'm serious. What's going on over there?"

"Whatever it is, I'm sure Russell can handle it. Everybody has a bad day, even Lena Horne, Dorothy Dandridge, Eartha Kitt—"

"All right. Stop it!" Clarice laughed, half-heartedly. "Helena did call me a few weeks ago and said she wanted to talk, but she never got back to me. I was a little surprised. We're not exactly girlfriends, you know. She didn't even mention it today."

"Whatever it is, you stay out of it," he said emphatically.

♣

The next day, Mose dropped Russell off at his front door, but instead of going in the house, Russell walked back up to North Avenue and down two blocks to the neighborhood watering hole, the Oasis.

The Oasis was a carbon copy of all the neighborhood bars that dotted the Baltimore City landscape. Most of the patrons were regular and knew each other. They were generally men seeking relief from 'the man', nagging wives, and girlfriends. They told war stories, complained about the plight of the black man, argued about politics—but never discussed religion—played pinochle, and got drunk. Some met their outside woman, but at a neighborhood bar other than their own.

It was still early and most of the regulars hadn't gotten off from work. Ignoring the barmaid, Lucille, with whom he usually engaged in meaningless banter, Russell ordered a beer at the counter and took it to a secluded booth in the back of the small bar. When he drained the glass, Lucille appeared.

"Kinda early for you, ain't it Russell, baby?

"I guess. Can I get another one?"

"You know you can get anything you want." She winked at Russell as she took the empty glass and sashayed to the bar for another draft.

Russell had already decided to confront Helena about what he suspected. It had been about two

111

weeks since the morning she was sick. He didn't think much about it at the time, but recently, he noticed the green uniform was not as big as it used to be. He didn't know how much, or how quickly pregnant women gained weight, but he was sure his wife was pregnant. And she had yet to tell him. What could possibly be the reason? The last time she told him it was because she didn't want to get his hopes up; but he was not going to accept that lame excuse this time. He trusted her, but what was she doing while he was in the hospital. For that matter, what did she do all day when he was working? And now that she worked part-time, who did she meet at work. By the time he downed his third beer and a shot of Jack Daniels, he was angry.

♣

Incensed by the lies the alcohol told his chemically altered brain, Russell burst into the front door with a vengeance. Ignoring the smell of pot roast waffling past his nose, he summoned his wife at the top of his voice. "Helena! Helena! Where are you? Where the hell are you, I said?"

"Who do you think you're yelling at?" Helena returned with equal volume as she appeared in the living room. "You sure do know how to mess up a girl's evening!"

Feeling like an idiot, Russell stood speechless, staring at Helena standing there with her arms folded and feet firmly planted, in a new black nightie. "Uh, yeah, hey baby. How you doing?"

"Better than you, that's for sure," she said, as she turned on her heels and started for the steps.

"Whoa, baby. Wait a minute. I need to talk to you—."

"And?" she called over her shoulder.

"What's going on? I mean, what are you doing?" a befuddled Russell stammered as he followed her up the stairs.

"Maybe if you had brought your butt home directly from work you could have found out. But no, you had to stop—at the Oasis, I presume—before you came home. What for?"

"What do you mean, 'what for'? What do you go to a bar for—" he said, starting to go on the defensive, but realized it was not in his best interest. Instead, he quickened his pace and caught up to Helena on the stairs. "Love that nightie," he purred, reaching under it and tapping Helena on the rump. "I smell something good cooking in the kitchen, too. Special occasion? Didn't mean to mess it up." Before Helena could say more than his name, Russell scooped her up and carried her to their room and deposited her on the bed.

"Russell" she began again, "we're having a baby!"

"I knew it. I knew it!" Russell said, as he walked back and forward beside the bed. "Oh," he said, as he got down on one knee in front of Helena and patted her stomach. "Guess I shouldn't have dropped you on the bed like that—sorry. It'll be all right, won't it?"

Helena laughed. "It'll be fine Russell."

"Did you tell your parents?"

"Not yet. I wanted to tell you first."

Russell kissed Helena, then got up and walked to the phone. "Let's call 'em now."

"No!" Helena said. She swung her legs off the bed and sat up.

Russell was taken aback by her response and shot her a quizzical look. "I mean not right now. We have some unfinished business to take care of," she said, patting the bed.

"You sure it's all right?"

"I'm sure. But let's wait awhile before we tell anybody—you know—just in case—"

"Okay, but I have a good feeling about this time. I know it'll be all right."

♣

Despite an early flash of euphoria, Helena brooded over the next two weeks, but successfully hid her melancholia from Russell. Finally tired of his nagging and unable to justify not doing so, she called her parents and told them the good news. Naturally, they were overjoyed at the prospect of their first grandchild. If her mother had any reservation about her conversation with Helena about Miss Ophelia, she didn't mention it.

Chapter Nineteen

Seven months later, April 1956

In keeping with the doctor's orders, Helena had spent the better part of her pregnancy in bed while her mother happily played nursemaid and housekeeper, helping insure Helena carried the baby to term. When her time came, two weeks early, Dr. Hill told her it had been a surprisingly easy delivery for a first time, high-risk pregnancy.

The slightly jaundiced Russell Ellis Sinclair Junior, came screaming into the world at seven pounds, ten ounces on April 22, 1956—a healthy weight for a baby who may have been two weeks early, which is why Dr. Hill doubted he was early. Of course, the new daddy would have preferred a hefty ten pounder, but he was as proud as a peacock as he handed out cigars—real ones and bubble gum ones—to his friends and family.

Despite Dr. Hill's pronouncements, Helena could not imagine the experience being any worse. Though her heart melted when they laid baby Russell on her chest, the sweetness of the moment did not completely erase the pain—emotional and physical—of the pregnancy. After delivery and recovery, she had slept fitfully, haunted in her dreams by a faceless man in a white lab coat, holding a baby at arm's length toward her.

Seems she had barely slept when the nurse brought baby Russell in for a feeding. First, she unwrapped the blanket and counted his fingers and toes—again, finding them all there. Then, with coaching from the nurse, she attempted the difficult task of what was supposed to be a natural process.

Soon after the nurse took baby Russell back to the nursery, a tired Helena started to doze again when a teddy bear-laden Natalie swooshed into the room.

"Wake-up sleepy head!" Natalie beckoned, dropping the stuffed toy on the foot of the bed and kissing Helena on the cheek." The ether worn off yet?" she inquired.

"What?" Helena asked, shaking her head as if to clear it and confirm what she was hearing.

"Yeah, the ether. You were talking out of your head yesterday, so I left. Besides, your family was here. Saw the baby. He looks just like Russell!"

"Russell?"

"Yeah, Russell. You know, his father. You sound surprised."

"Surprised? Of course not! Why would I be surprised? It's just to me, newborns don't look like anybody except little old people—wrinkled, toothless, sometimes bald—that's all," she said with forced gaiety.

Natalie gave Helena a curious look. "I was just kidding—I mean, not about him looking like Russell, but about you being surprised—" her voice trailed off as she stared at Helena. "He's a scrawny little thing, and bright!"

"Natalie, he has a little jaundice. It's common, but you know our babies always start out light. He'll get his color in a few days."

"Not my problem," Natalie mumbled under her breath. "But, how are you? When do you go home? How is the new daddy?"

"Whoa, Natalie!" Helena laughed. "Fine. Tomorrow. Fine."

Natalie plopped down in the chair next to the bed. "How long is your mother staying?"

"About a month," Helena replied with an air of uncertainty. *Guess I'll know by then whether to pack up and go back home with her.*

117

"You know I'm just around the corner if you need me. My mother wouldn't do that for me. Of course, I don't intend to give her a reason to have to—you know what I mean—not until I find my Russell."

For a few seconds, an uneasy silence filled the room as the two of them got lost in their own weighty thoughts.

Chapter Twenty

Six months later, October 1956...

The room was a peaceful robin's egg blue and the night-light caste Helena's shadow on the wall. She was glad her mother had insisted she put a rocking chair in the tiny bedroom that became the baby's nursery. She sat gently rocking Russ Jr, which soothed him. He was a fussy baby and kept her up most nights, the effect of calming blue walls lost on him.

Helena had been sure she would resent—even hate—Russ Jr, but he was an innocent victim of her unfortunate circumstance. She didn't come to that conclusion easily, but it was difficult not to love a warm, well-feed, freshly diapered baby, who slept peacefully on her chest. When he fussed, she hummed a tune that was in her head, but that she didn't know the origin of, or when she had learned it.

Russ Jr was still very pale, but his hair had darkened, and his once loose curls had begun to coil tighter. He looked like his daddy—Russell. Or at least, Helena thought so. She couldn't decide if it was actually true or if her brain willed her to believe it. She sniffed Russ Jr's sweet baby's breath and rested her cheek against his head. Humming the unknown lullaby, she nodded off until a hushed voice called her name.

"Helena, Helena," Russell said in a loud whisper, poking his head in the door. "Put the baby down and come to bed."

"Shush, Russell. You'll wake him up."

"Come to bed," Russell said a little louder. "He's asleep."

"Not in deep sleep—" she said. When Russell started to open the door wider, she got up. "Okay, Russell. Be quiet I'll put him down. Go on back to bed."

"No. I'm waiting for you," Russell insisted, his voice almost at normal volume.

Helena put Russ Jr in his crib and maneuvered around the furniture in the crowded room. Russell held the door and she slid by him. "I don't know why you had to get up—"

"To keep you from sleeping another night in the rocking chair. That's gotta stop. You hear me?"

"You know he's a fussy baby."

"Yeah. Well, I'm a fussy baby too, and something's gotta give. And tonight, that's something is you," he said, shoving her slightly.

"What are you doing Russell? Stop it."

"Shush, you'll wake the baby," he said sarcastically.

Helena never had a reason to fear her husband, but she suddenly felt threatened. He had hardly ever raised his voice, let alone raised his hand at her. She quickly walked to their bedroom with Russell close behind. Before she realized it, he grabbed her from behind and picked her up.

"Russell, what are you doing?" Helena asked.

Without saying a word, Russell walked to the bed and unceremoniously dropped Helena. Before she could catch her breath, he kneeled beside the bed and put one arm across her chest to pin her down. Suddenly, she had flashbacks of that dreadful July day. She bit her lip to keep from screaming, but wildly swung her arms and kicked her legs.

"Stop it! Stop it, Helena. What the hell's the matter with you? I'm not going to hurt you. Calm down."

"You threw me on the bed," Helena hissed trying to hold back tears.

"This ain't the first time I threw you on the bed. I just want to talk."

"Like this?" Helena said nodding toward the arm that restrained her as she tried to get up.

"Yes," Russell replied without removing his arm. "I want to know what's wrong with you. Don't you love me anymore?"

"Let me up, please."

"No. Not yet. Answer my question. What's wrong?"

"Nothing—I don't know. I'm just tired—the baby—"

"Don't give me that baby, shit. I don't want to hear it. It's been weeks since we made love and tonight's the night."

"Russell, please. Not like this."

"What do you mean, 'not like this'?"

"It's like you're forcing me—like you're going to rape—"

With that, Russell stood up. "You've lost your mind. A man can't rape his wife. I don't want to make you do nothing you don't want to do. I'm sorry that's what you think." He turned and headed for the door.

"Russell, I'm sorry. I do love you. I need some time—"

Russell stopped and turned slightly. "You keep saying that. Time for what?"

"I don't know. I need to see Dr. Hill. Maybe my hormones are out of whack or something—"

"Yeah. Something is out of whack, all right," he said, before descending the steps.

Helena rolled over to her side of the bed and buried her head in her pillow to muffle the sobs. She thought she heard Russ Jr, but she was too distraught to move. *Please God help me. I don't know what to do.*

Chapter Twenty-one

Two months later, January 1957...

The Oasis was relatively quiet because the usual Friday night crowd had not begun to file in. The jukebox was low, and the barmaids were idle. Russell took a sip of his National Bohemian Beer, and with his eyes closed, rested his head against the back of his favorite booth. Before too long, he got a whiff of a light, but cheap, perfume and felt the soft contours of an ample warm body pressing against him. He knew instantly it was Lucille.

"What's the matter, baby?" Lucille cooed.

He rolled his shoulder to dislodge her, but before he could answer, he heard a shrill voice calling his name. "Russell. Hey, Russell!"

Reluctantly, Lucille slid out of the booth, but stood leaning against it as Natalie bolted to the back of the club.

"Hi, Natalie," Russell responded. "A little early for you ain't it?"

"Not really," Natalie responded, "but then I don't have a wife and baby at home." With her hand on her hip, she stared intently at Lucille. "Don't you have some customers to wait on?"

Lucille sucked her teeth, rolled her eyes and walked away.

"What's with the smart-ass remarks?" Russell asked, as Natalie slid into the booth opposite him.

"Just keeping you out of trouble," she said.

"Thanks," Russell said sarcastically. "First, I don't need your protection," he said, enumerating his position by pointing his index finger. "And second," he continued, raising his middle finger, "it ain't none of your business."

"Yeah, you're right," Natalie said, swatting at his hand. "But I don't like that hussy, and Helena is my girl."

"Look, Natalie. Lucille is harmless. I know you're a good friend to me and Helena, but you over stepped your bounds. Butt out. Better yet, clear out. I'm waiting for Mose."

"Say what?" Natalie said, as she folded her arms and sat back in the booth.

"Go Natalie. Just go. How 'bout, if I say please?"

Reluctantly, Natalie got up, and as she turned to leave, she bumped square into Mose.

"Hi Nat—" Moses started as Natalie brushed by him in a huff. "What's up with her?" he asked Russell, as he slid into the booth.

"Got me," Russell responded. "Hey, Lucille. Can I get two more Natty Bohs back here?" he yelled.

"I can't hang out too long," Russell said, as a different barmaid brought them their beers. "I gotta babysit while Helena gets her knots busted."

"Babysit?" Mose laughed. "You gettin' paid?"

"Paid? Hell no. It's my own kid. Why should I get paid?"

"Precisely, Youngster," Mose said. "You don't babysit your own kid. You take care of it. That's your job."

"Yeah, yeah. Mose, sometimes I wish you would stop trying to be my father."

Mose sipped his beer. "Just tellin' it like it is. Think I'll get a burger," he said, as he signaled for a barmaid.

Absently, Russell played with the salt shaker on the table. "I guess I spoke too soon. I need some fatherly wisdom. How did Clarice act after Mose Jr was born?"

"What do you mean, 'how did she act?' Besides, that was almost five years ago."

"Russ Jr gets all of Helena's attention. Half the time, she won't even let me touch him. Hell, half the time she wouldn't even let me touch her. I don't get it."

"With new mothers, it takes time—I guess. Somethin' about hormones. I don't remember what went on with Clarice."

"Mose, you'd remember if she cut you off." Russell smirked.

"You right about that, Youngster."

126

"Russ Jr is nine months old. How much time does she need? Time for what?"

"I wish I knew, Youngster. And if you show up drunk tonight, she ain't gonna let you *baby-sit* for sure."

"As usual, you're right, but something's gotta give. When I'm playing with him, she watches me like a hawk. Like I'm going to do something to him. She's just not the same Helena."

"Talk to her. You ever think of that?" Mose said, as he took a bite out of his burger. "I can't stay long."

"I don't know where to start. It's almost like she dares me to say anything. Are you babysitting, I mean, keeping Mose Jr tonight while Clarice is at work?"

"Yeah. Why don't I bring him around and we can talk some more. Maybe I'll have it figured out by then," he said, lifting the hamburger bun to examine the contents of his sandwich.

Russell tossed some bills on the table and got up. "Okay, I'm going. See you later." He scanned the bar to avoid running into Lucille. Seeing the coast was clear, he quickly made his way out of the Oasis.

♣

Both little boys were asleep—Russ Jr splayed on his back in his playpen and Mose Jr on a pallet of blankets next to it. The grown-up boys stared blankly at them, now sipping soda instead of beer.

"I didn't know one little baby could raise so much hell," Russell said, shaking his head.

"Misses his momma I guess," was Mose's reply.

"That's what I'm talking about. Helena's got that boy ruined already," Russell responded, just a little annoyed.

"Don't let her do to him what Clarice is doing to Raymond."

"How is she doing something to him when he's never around?"

"When he is around, she acts like he's going to break or something."

With a knowing nod, Russell shifted his weight on the sofa while he carefully considered his next question. "You ever meet Raymond's daddy?" he asked, trying to sound matter-of-fact.

"No. Clarice don't ever want to talk about him. Fact is, her momma and daddy don't even know who he is."

"You lying, Mose," an incredulous Russell said, sitting up on the edge of his chair.

"Why would I lie about a thing like that, Youngster?"

"Man, you gotta be a little curious. What's the big secret?"

"Ask me no questions, and I'll tell you no lies. Clarice don't talk about it and I don't ask. So, if you don't mind, it ain't none of your business. Besides, I think you got problems of your own."

"Nothing I can't handle—"

"Yeah? Changed your tune since the Oasis, huh? Speaking of the Oasis, what's with you and Lucille?"

"Me and Lucille? Nothing! Maybe you need to ask Lucille what her problem is."

"The way I see it, Youngster. You ripe for picking."

"Now you got observations? I asked you about my wife, and you talking about a barmaid?"

"Not any barmaid. I'm talking about Lucille," Mose said, laughing.

Russell shushed him as Russ Jr turned over in the play pen.

Chapter Twenty-two

Ressy hated these things, these dinner parties. They kept her late into the evening, increased the number of white people she had to serve and smile at, and brought her face to face with Connor Monahan III, whom she despised. It was his sixtieth birthday and he had come home from New York on a rare visit to celebrate. To Reesy's delight, a caterer and his staff were hired to prepare the food, but they still needed her to show them around the kitchen, help serve, prepare the drinks, and assist with the clean-up.

Connor III, an imposing figure, had managed to keep at bay most of the girth that comes with his age. His barber left just enough grey at his temples after his dye jobs to achieve a distinguished and charming but not old effect. At the ripe old age of sixty, he was still dashing with enough money and influence to make him even more appealing.

The ten dinner guests, Baltimore old money, were in the sitting room having before-dinner cocktails when Connor III made his way to the kitchen. Ressy was removing wine classes from the dish washer when he appeared in the doorway. "Ressy, it's so good to see you. Do you ever age?" he asked with just a slight lingering of the southern accent he tried desperately to lose.

"Good evening, Connor," Ressy said. She dared call him by his first name, which Connor III allowed, as long as she was out of earshot of other people. "I'm fine. How have you been? Shouldn't you be with your guests?" she asked without looking up from her task.

"Trying to get rid of me, already? I just wanted to know about your family," Connor III said, putting his hands in his pockets and leaning against the refrigerator.

The last thing Ressy wanted to do was engage in small talk with her employer. She breathed a sigh of relief when she heard the soft clicking of Mrs. Monahan's cane against the foyer's marble floor. "There you are Connor," she said with false gaiety. "I know you're not bothering Ressy, are you?"

Ressy didn't miss the brief, but icy stare Maureen Monahan shot at her husband.

"No ma'am," Ressy replied. "He just asked about the family, and I was shooing him out."

"I'm sure he did. Come Connor," she said, taking him by the arm. "The caterers are waiting to serve the soup." With that, she led him into the dining room.

Ressy watched them leave and breathed a sigh of relief.

Chapter Twenty-three

Even though she busied herself with fixing Russell's lunch, Helena kept a watchful eye on him as he fed the baby his morning oatmeal.

"Come on little man. Eat your cereal for daddy," Russell said in sing-sung baby talk.

"Why don't you put him in his high chair and feed him?" Helena asked, trying to sound matter-of-fact.

"'Cause I like to do it with him on my lap." Russell said, putting a spoon full of cereal in Russ Jr's mouth. "Your momma thinks I don't know what I'm doing," he said, pretending to be whispering in the baby's ear.

"Russell, you know that's not true," Helena protested. "What makes you say that?"

"What makes me say that? You gotta be kidding. You watch me like a hawk. That's why I say that. And I'm getting a little tired of it. This is my son, too, you know. I'm not going to do anything to hurt him. Here. Take him," Russell said, standing up and pushing Russ Jr into her arms. "Feed him your *damn* self. I'll fix my own lunch."

Angrily, he shoved two sandwiches into a brown bag and stormed out of the kitchen.

"Russell. I'm not doing that. I'm sorry. I trust you. Please don't be mad," Helena pleaded, as she followed Russell.

"I don't want to hear it. I keep telling you something's wrong, but you won't listen. I've had enough." He walked out the front door and slammed it hard enough to rattle the windows.

Hastily, Helena put Russ Jr in the playpen she kept in the living room, and went outside, only to see Russell walking up the street. She assumed he was going to wait for Mose on the corner instead of in front of the house. She wanted to go after him, but she was in her housecoat and she certainly couldn't leave the baby unattended.

Once at the corner, Helena saw Russell turn around, so she wildly waved her arms as if she were hailing a taxi, hoping to get his attention. The distance was not great, and she knew he saw her but he turned his back. Dejected, Helena when back into the house and found Russ Jr wailing at the top of his lungs.

"Shhh, little boy," she said, as she picked him up. Mommy's here. I'll never leave you." She shifted him to her hip and went into the dining room to call Natalie.

"Hello," Natalie said hurriedly.

"Hey, Nat. How you doing?"

"Helena? Fine. What's wrong? Why are you calling me this time of the morning? I'm about to head out to work."

"I know. Sorry. Need a favor. Do you think Aunt Loretta would keep Russ Jr for me for a couple of hours this afternoon?"

"I'm sure she would, but you have to ask her. Call her on her phone. You got her number? There's nothing wrong, is there?"

"I do—no, nothing wrong."

"Good. I gotta run. Call her. Talk to you later."

"Okay, bye." As soon as she hung up from Natalie, she dialed Aunt Loretta.

"Hello. Your dime, start talking." Loretta laughed.

Helena always laughed when she called Natalie's Aunt Loretta. She couldn't imagine her very prim and proper mother answering the phone that way. Because Helena and Natalie were so close, Helena called Loretta 'Aunt,' too.

"Hi, Aunt Loretta. It's me, Helena. How are you?"

"Just fine. Natalie said you would call. What can I do for you?"

"If you could keep Russ Jr for me from about eleven until about two this afternoon, I'll sing at your wedding."

"Ain't gonna be no weddings, so you better come up with a better offer than that. But sure, I'll keep the little rascal," she laughed. "Just bring him and his stuff around here."

"Yes ma'am, and thanks so much."

"No problem. See you then."

Helena packed Russ Jr's diaper bag and headed for Aunt Loretta's. From there she was going to catch a cab to Russell's construction site off Pratt Street, and meet him when he was on lunch break—usually around noon. She had dressed carefully, made up her face, and put on perfume. She had to do something to get her marriage back on track, but she gave little thought to how she was going to fix what was going on inside of her.

Helena got out of the cab on the corner, opposite the site, so she could figure out which direction she needed to go. It wasn't long before the whistle blew and men of all shapes and sizes laid down jack hammers, torches, and all sorts of clanging, banging tools, emerged from scaffolding and a maze of two by fours, and headed for a nonhazardous place to eat lunch from brown bags and metal boxes. With hard hats and uniforms, it was difficult to distinguish one man from another. A small wave headed for the deli behind Helena, cat-calling and whistling as they made their way around her. *Wrong corner*, she thought, as she craned her neck for Russell. She spotted Mose and ran toward him.

"Mose. Where's Russell?"

Caught off guard, Mose was momentarily speechless. "Helena? Something wrong? What are you doing here?"

"Excuse me, Mose. That's none of your business. No, nothing's wrong."

"I'm sorry. I'm just concerned. I mean this is unusual and Youngster was—"

"Mose, do you know where he eats?"

"Yeah, sure. He's probably on the parking lot. He eats in the car sometimes—I'll take you there. You know you shouldn't be in a hardhat area—"

"I know. Thanks, Mose. I didn't mean to get smart with you."

"That's all right. Follow me. It's about two blocks. We don't have much time." Mose hesitated for a minute and scratched his head before he headed toward the parking lot. He managed to pull a sandwich out of his lunch box and ate as they walked. Helena followed two steps behind.

As they approached their destination, Helena saw a small group of men, heads down, huddled in a circle. "Aye!" she heard one of them yell. "Sinclair, your luck's run out again. You out?" Helena stopped dead in her tracks.

"Wait here," Mose said. He walked over to the men shooting dice and called Russell.

"What, Mose? Don't you see I'm busy?" Russell said, annoyed.

"Yeah, but somebody is here to see you. Think you better get *unbusy*."

"What?" Russell said, walking from the far side of the circle.

Helena didn't know who was more shocked— Russell or her.

"Helena, what are you—something happened? Where's the baby—?" Russell said, as he walked toward Helena.

"The baby's fine. After this morning, I thought I'd surprise you and meet you for lunch to say I'm sorry—but it doesn't look like it was a good idea."

"No, it wasn't. I mean I appreciate the thought, but this isn't the place—"

"Yeah, I see that. You shoot craps every day?"

"Don't change the subject. This ain't about me shooting craps."

"I guess not. I'll see you later." As she started to walk away, one of the men asked Russell if he was coming back to the game.

"No, man. I'm done," Russell said, as he caught up to Helena and grabbed her arm. "I'm sorry I stormed out this morning. I'm sorry about the game—"

"I should have stayed my behind home. Ignorance is bliss. I'll see you later, Russell." She pulled away from him and walked in the direction she had come.

Mose shrugged his shoulders, leaned against the nearest car and finished his lunch. Russell just watched her go.

Chapter Twenty-four

Later that week, when Russell walked into the Oasis, he joined a group of men arguing over the NFL Championship game in which the New York Giants beat the Chicago Bears 47 to 7. After he tired of the conversation, he headed for his favorite booth.

As he sipped his favorite brew, he had a pity party. In his mind, Helena had made some feeble attempt to fix the problem of intimacy in their marriage, but it just wasn't the same. She claimed she went to see Dr. Hill for some kind of medication, but if she did, it wasn't working. Then there was that crazy stunt she pulled coming to the job site. The guys hadn't let him live that one down. Some called him a stud, having his wife chase him down, and others said he was whipped. *I'm a stud all right, without a filly.*

He drained his glass and looked around for a barmaid, conscious of the fact he hadn't seen Lucille. After nobody appeared, he walked to the bar to place his order.

"Who's on tonight?" he asked the guy on the stool next to him.

"Best I can tell, the usual crew," was his reply.

Hearing that, Russell headed back to his booth without ordering another beer. He sat down and closed his eyes.

"What's for you sugar? The usual?" Lucille's familiar voice purred.

"Hey, Lucille. How you doing?"

"Fine, good lookin'. You want a Natty Boh?"

"No. Don't think so. How about a JW Red, straight up. Beer chaser. In the bottle."

"Whoa. JW? That's a big boy's drink."

"I'm a big boy."

"I'll take your word for it. Can't prove it by me."

"Maybe you could."

Lucille leaned across the table to give Russell a full view of her generous cleavage in her low-cut blouse. "What are you talkin' about? You wouldn't tease me, would you?"

"My drink, Lucille. My drink."

"You're full of it, Russell Sinclair," Lucille said, visibly annoyed. As she left the table, she poked out her hip and patted her butt.

Russell just laughed. When Lucille brought his drinks, she slammed the beer bottle down on the table and Russell grabbed her arm. "What time do you get off tonight?"

"What's it to you?"

"What time do you get off, Lucille? I'll wait for you."

"I have to close tonight. You not jiving me, are you?"

"No. I'll wait for you."

"You won't be sorry," Lucille whispered.

Russell downed his shot and took his beer up front to hang out with the guys.

As it got close to closing time, Russell made sure Natalie was not in the Oasis. Instead of staying in the bar, he decided to wait for Lucille in the storeroom. He didn't have to wait too long before a buoyant Lucille appeared.

"Everything's done," Lucille said, as she came through the storeroom door. "How are we going to do this? I don't live far. We can catch a cab together. Nobody's on the street now anyway."

"Okay, but come here first," Russell slurred in his slightly inebriated state.

Lucille walked over to him and pressed her body against his. Russell encircled her waist, backed her against the wall, and tore at her blouse.

"Russell. Not here. Not like this," Lucille protested as Russell groped her.

"Don't talk, Lucille," Russell said, as his mouth and tongue explored her breast like a hungry newborn. He raised her skirt, pulled down her panties and probed her femininity.

"Russell. Down boy. Not here."

"Shut up. I'm at the point of no return. Undo my pants."

Without further protest, Lucille deftly complied. "Do you have a raincoat?" she asked. Her hands found out the answer as Russell nodded. "You came prepared," she whispered.

Consumed with animal lust, Russell entered her roughly. Lucille moaned first from pleasure, then pain and begged Russell to stop. Only after he was spent, did he comply.

"I'm sorry, Lucille. I didn't mean to hurt you," he said, fumbling with his pants.

"Well, you did. Didn't know you were so hard up. You shouldna waited so long. I was ready anytime you asked. I'll call a cab and we can go to my place and do it right."

"Maybe another time—I can't go now—"

"What do you mean, you can't go now? That's it? Smack, bam, thank you ma'am. I thought you were different, but you just like all them other niggers. Just a prettier package. Get the hell out!"

"I'm sorry. It was a mistake. I'm drunk."

"Mistake, huh? Was it a mistake when you put that rubber on? Was you drunk then? I said get the fuck out."

Russell found his jacket on the floor, put it on, and slipped out into the January night. He was a mess. His clothes were disheveled, and he smelled of booze, cheap perfume, smoke, sweat, and sex. The cold air helped clear his head and he thought he heard footsteps behind him, but he was not alarmed. His neighborhood was safe—usually. It was not until the footsteps grew louder and seemed closer did Russell look over his shoulder. Suddenly, a beefy, strong arm put him in a headlock. Instinctively, Russell attempted to elbow his assailant, but the attacker let him go before the blow could land.

"Sinclair, man I told you 'bout walkin' these streets drunk," Scottie laughed. He put up his dukes and bounced on his toes. "You almost got me, but you ain't that quick."

"I don't see a damn thing funny Scottie," Russell said. Adrenalin still pumping, he put both hands in Scottie's chest and shoved him. "Don't you have anything better to do besides runnin' up on somebody this time of the morning?"

"I'm on my j-o-b," Scottie said, regaining his footing. "What *you* doing out here? Closin' the bar, huh?"

"None of your business, Scottie. Besides, I live around here."

"Helpin' Lucille close the bar? Yeah, Nipper helped her close it a few times himself."

"What's that supposed to mean?"

"You ain't stupid, Sinclair. Lucille is one of Nipper's women and he don't like niggers messin' with his women or his money. You treadin' on dangerous ground."

"I don't know what—"

"Okay, play dumb, but you gonna get yo'self hurt. I told you before, I like you. That's why my blade's still in my pocket and not in your gut. Consider this a warning. Nipper don't mind you being in his debt, 'long as you make the weekly. In fact, he hopes you stay in debt, but you behind on your weekly. And don't get any ideas about Lucille. You can't afford her. Consider this time a free one."

Just as Russell opened his mouth to speak, a car stopped at the curb and the passenger door swung open.

"Better get home, Sinclair," Scottie said, as he climbed into the car. The driver made a u-turn and sped off on screeching tires.

Breathing heavily, Russell leaned against the nearest house to regain his composure. He hung his head between his legs and rested his elbows on his knees.

Why didn't I know Lucille was one of Nipper's? But why should I know? I never saw her at any of the games. Why the hell did I have to screw her anyway? I got caught up. Musta lost my mind. What am I going to tell Helena? Tell Helena? Don't think so. Nothing. If she had been doing what—that's no excuse and you know it, Russell. But I need my wife to be a wife. His head started to throb. He straightened up and swiftly walked the rest of the way home.

When he reached his house, he paused before he put the key in the door and tried to figure out what he would say to Helena if she were awake. Not that he didn't stay out late some Saturday nights, but his guilt made him sure she would question him. For once, he hoped Helena would be asleep in the nursery. He quietly entered the house and walked to the bottom of the stairs where he stopped to listen.

Hearing the soft rhythmic thud of the rocking chair, he breathed a sigh of relief, took off his shoes and headed up the steps. Midway up, he froze to the sound of Helena humming. The nursery was at the top of the steps, across a tiny hallway. To the right of it, was a second bedroom that extended a little way down the hallway. Next to that, was the master bedroom and the bathroom. The bathroom was at the end of the hall, directly opposite the nursery. All of the rooms were within a few steps of each other, and there was no way to get to the bathroom or his bedroom without being seen from the nursery. His goose was cooked.

"Russell?" Helena whispered.

"Yeah. Gotta go to the John."

"Nothing. Go."

A sliver of illumination from the nightlight came through the slightly opened nursery door. Russell skulked down the hall without peeping in to say anything to Helena. He quickly went into the bathroom and locked the door, something neither of them ever did. He doubted Helena would come to scrub his back like she used to do, but given his luck of late, he wasn't taking any chances.

Russell tore off his clothes as if they had offended him and dropped them on the floor. Then he ran a tub, got in before it filled, and scrubbed himself with a vengeance. While his brain was trying to shake off the memory of the evening, his body had a mind of its own and his need was still evident. *Hell, I didn't bring my pajamas in here.* When he finished bathing, he got out of the tub, grabbed a towel, wrapped it around the body that was betraying him, and listened at the door. Helena was still in the rocking chair, humming. He hurried down the hall, found his pjs and got into bed. After a short time, he drifted off into a fitful sleep.

Chapter Twenty-five

The next day was Sunday and the smell of coffee and bacon waffled through the house. Russ Jr sat in his highchair gnawing and drooling on a piece of Melba toast. Helen filled a cup and sat down in front of the baby's high chair.

"Okay, little man," she said. "Mommy's going upstairs for a minute, and then I'll come back and feed you. Don't fuss. I'll be right back."

She stomped loudly up the stairs to be sure to wake Russell if he wasn't already awake. He wasn't, and was snoring loudly. Helena shook him like a dirty rug. "Russell. Russell. Wake up."

She rolled her eyes as Russell sat up and put his hand out, she assumed, expecting the usual Anacin and glass of water she gave him when she suspected he had a hangover. "I guess you're not going to church today. You need to get your funky clothes off the bathroom floor and do your laundry. While you're at it, wash out the tub. You didn't drain it last night—I mean *this morning*—when you came in."

She turned around to go and Russell grabbed her arm. "Helena, I need to talk you, please."

"I don't think so, Russell. I'm not talking to you today, so let go of my arm."

"Don't you care about us—about me—anymore?"

"Strange you should ask that question."

"Why? I'm not the one avoiding you. You hardly give me the time of day."

"That's not true. You're exaggerating, and you know it." Helena leaned toward the door. "I hear little Russ. I left him in his highchair." Russell let go of her arm, and she left the room.

"That's part of the problem—" she heard Russell say, as she hurried down the stairs. She found Russ Jr leaning across the highchair tray, straining to see around the kitchen door. He was whimpering and banging on the tray with his spoon.

"Here I come, baby. Big boys don't cry," she said, as she lifted him out of the chair and shifted him to her hip. She went to the stove and put some grits on a plate with a strip of bacon. When she turned to put the plate on the table, Russell was standing in the doorway.

She was startled by his presence. A wave of emptiness swept over her seeing him standing there barefoot and topless in his pajamas.

"Didn't mean to scare you," Russell said. "You're awfully jumpy these days. Did you tell Dr. Hill that, too?"

"I didn't go," she said, sitting down.

"What you mean, you didn't go? You led me to believe you did."

"He couldn't tell me anything I didn't already know."

"Really? So school me. What's your problem?"

"*My problem?* I think it's our problem."

"If it is, I can't fix it by myself, especially if I don' know what the problem is. So what's wrong?"

"I told you. A hormone imbalance—"

"I thought there was medicine for that, but you didn't even go to the doctor. That tells me a lot. For whatever reason, you don't want to fix this. I said we need to talk."

"That's not true, and you know it. But let me ask you something. Why were you tipping in this morning? You're a husband and a father and you got no busy being in the street that time of the morning. If you came home at a decent hour, maybe we could have talked yesterday."

"Now you trying to make this about me? Maybe I didn't have anything to talk about yesterday. Anyway, you're not available."

Helena sprung out of her chair and put Russ Jr on the floor. She watched him crawl toward the living room before she approached her husband. "What did you just say to me Russell Sinclair?" she hissed. "What does that mean, I'm not available?" she asked, as she got into his face. "I said, what does that mean?" she repeated, fighting back angry tears.

Russell turned away from her intense gaze. "Nothing. It means nothing."

"Who is she, Russell? Who is *available*?"

"There is no she," Russell replied quietly.

"You're a liar! I smelled your clothes. They stunk of cheap perfume and musk," Helena said, pummeling his chest with her fists. "You're a liar!"

Russell garbed her arms. "Stop, Helena. You're getting yourself upset for nothing. Stop."

"Let go of me," she said with tight-lip determination. Russell released her and backed against the wall.

Angry and hurt, Helena swiftly walked to the living room to search for Russ Jr as a way out of the escalating situation. "Russ. Russ Jr Where are you? Mommy's looking for you." She turned to the sound of his babbling and found him half way up the steps. Fearing he might fall, Helena darted up behind him.

"Oh, my goodness. Russ Jr you know better than to crawl up these steps by yourself," she said, as she snatched him from the stairs and sat down.

Russell came out of the kitchen, climbed the stairs and sat one step below them. "Boys will be boys, ain't that right, partner?" he laughed uncomfortably. "Why don't you leave him with me while you go to church? We'll make out just fine," he said, taking the baby from Helena. "It'll give you a break."

"Yeah, boys will be boys, won't they?" The sarcasm curled her lips.

"Am I going to get smart-ass comments from you all day?"

"No. If you remember, I have nothing more to say to you today."

"Just today?" he smirked. "Have it your way but go to church. It always makes you feel better. Russ Jr will be just fine here with me. Won't you, big boy?" He turned his back to Helena and told Russ Jr to climb on. Then off they went, down the stairs, with a conflicted Helena looking on.

"He didn't eat his breakfast yet—" Helena called after them.

"Yeah, yeah. I'll see that he eats, or I just may starve him to death."

Heart-broken and weary, Helena dropped her head in her lap. She was sure Russell told her a bald-faced lie, but she was even more demoralized because she believed he had committed an act worthy of a denial. This was the final nail in the coffin, and she had no choice but to go through with her plans. She managed to get herself up and went to get dressed. She wasn't much in the mood for church, but she needed to get out of the house. *What was it they said to visitors at church? Maybe some song, or prayer, or the Word will lift your spirits and meet you at your need.* She could only hope.

♣

Russell put Russ Jr in his highchair and absently fed him his breakfast. *My God. I can't believe this mess I've gotten myself into. How could I do this to Helena? Maybe if she hadn't come at me like she did and let me talk when I asked her, I would have told her the truth and asked for her forgiveness. But the lie just rolled of my tongue like butter on a hot biscuit. She's gotta know how much I love her, and I never want to hurt her. It meant nothing. It was just ... sex. But, I can't tell her....*

The sound of Russ Jr pounding the highchair with his sippy cup snapped Russell out of his revelry. "Okay, little man. Looks like you've had enough. Let's go read the paper." He freed Russ Jr from the chair, put him under his arm like a sack of potatoes, carried him to the living room, and deposited him in his playpen—a place Russ Jr didn't want to be. He immediately started to cry.

"What's the matter with you?" Russell asked leaning over the playpen. "Your mommy got you rotten. All right. I'll take you out, but you gotta let me read the paper. Okay? Okay!"

Russell took the crying baby from his playpen and gently tossed him in the air. Russ Jr responded with that infectious, gurgling belly laugh babies have. Russell couldn't help but laugh too as he sat the baby his knee. "All right. That was fun. Boy, I'll be glad when you get some color." With Helena out of the way getting ready for church, father and son shared a rare moment of bonding.

When Helen came downstairs, Russell diverted the baby's attention so Helena could slip pass without being seen. Otherwise, Russ Jr would have wailed to go with her. Russell nodded at her as she headed for the door, but she averted her eyes.

That set the tone for the rest of the day; they barely said two words to each other, even over dinner.

Chapter Twenty-six

The gloom of a January Monday afternoon had managed to seep into the house and cast a dreary veil over its chief occupant. Helena pulled down the shades in the living room and switched on a lamp. The extra minute of daylight added every day since the Winter Solstice made no difference. Without lights at 4:00 p.m. in the afternoon, the house was dark. The dark matched her mood.

Helena surveyed the suitcases by the door and mentally inventoried what she had packed. Russ Jr's things took up the most space. It wasn't going to be a fun trip with a ten-month-old, but she had no choice. Besides, her mother couldn't wait to have the two of them come visit. She had neglected to tell her mother the trip might be more than a visit, but she would cross that bridge when she got to there. Helena knew she would have to have some things shipped, but that was to be dealt with later as well.

The carefully written note was on the coffee table, and the cab was to be there shortly. Even though it would be the decent thing to do, she couldn't bear telling Russell face-to-face she was leaving, and she wanted desperately to avoid a confrontation. She had planned to be out of the house earlier, but Russ Jr had been fussy, and she couldn't stay focused on the packing.

At the moment, he was sleeping peacefully on the sofa. Leaving was not a spur-of-the-moment idea, but the plan in her head had not translated into action until the last minute. She paced nervously and prayed the cab would hurry. She froze in her tracks as she heard Russell's key turning in the door. Ordinarily, she could set her watch by the time he got home but today, of all days, he was early. She knew she would never forget the shocked look on Russell's face as he stepped out of the vestibule into the living room.

"What the hell is going on here?" he asked, surveying the room. "Where do you think you're going, Helena?"

"I—we—are going to North Carolina for a few days to see my parents," she stammered.

"A few days, with all this shit? I don't think so. I don't think you're going any place," Russell said, as he took a menacing step toward Helena.

Instinctively, she backed up. "Yes, I am. I need some time to think some things over."

"What things? I come in drunk one night and you accuse me of messing around, and then you pack-up to leave me?" an incredulous Russell asked.

"You've come in drunk more than one night. It's not about that. It's not about you having another woman, which I am sure of. It's about me. But now that you find it necessary to screw other women, you made my decision easier."

"I told you, I'm not screwing anybody else. That's a joke—I'm not even screwing you."

"That's the first sign—"

"Oh, so that's an automatic? If it's not you, it has to be somebody? If you think that—if I'm seeing somebody else—it's your fault. I made what decision easier? Before Saturday, you had already decided to leave? Why?"

"Russell, I need to go. I'll call you when I'm ready to talk," Helena said, tearfully.

"Just like that. No answers. You're giving up on me—our marriage—what we had without even discussing it with me? You're not taking my son, but you can go."

Russell picked up Russ Jr from the couch. Helena bit her lip and choked back the words that were trying to tumble out of her mouth. Instead of speaking, she quickly picked up the note from the coffee table and tore it in pieces. It contained all the details she couldn't verbalize, but she changed her mind about leaving it.

"Go Helena. But you're going without him."

"Make sense, Russell. You can't keep the baby and work, too. Let me have him."

"Make sense? Make sense, you say. None of this makes sense. You got a lot of damn nerve. Was that the note you were leaving for me? I can't believe it. You were going to go and just leave me a note. What did I do to you to make you treat me this way?"

"I can't explain it now, but you'll understand soon enough. Please give me my baby, Russell."

"You're lucky I'm not a violent man, or I'd beat your ass right here and right now. Take *your* baby," he said, then sat Russ Jr back on the couch.

The baby was crying in the midst of the commotion. With arms outstretched, Russ Jr reached for his father, and dabbled, "Da da da da."

At that moment, Helena's already aching heart, bruised by guilt, seemingly broke in half. Never mind that pediatricians say, 'da da' is one of a baby's first sounds. But hearing her baby only accentuated the gravity of the situation.

For a few seconds, Helena and Russell stared at each other in icy silence. In the heat of the argument, neither one of them heard the cab horn nor the driver banging on the front door. Russell, paralyzed in place, stared blankly at the door, while Helena answered it. "I'm sorry. We didn't hear your horn, sir, but I'll be right out."

"Helena, can we just talk about it? I mean, let's talk, and if you still want to go, I'll call another cab."

"No, Russell. I have to leave. I need to think some things out."

"Just like that, huh?"

"I'm sorry Russell, but you'll understand soon. Could you help—?"

Russell stared blankly at Helena as she picked up the baby and zipped him in his snowsuit.

"You planned to leave before I got home, so pretend I'm not here," Russell said softly. Then he kissed Russ Jr on the forehead and went up the steps.

Helena looked forlornly around the room and quietly slipped out the door. She cried all the way to the train station.

♣

Russell didn't know how long he had been sitting on the side of the bed, but the house had grown darker and colder, and he wasn't sure if the coldness was physical or mental. The entire afternoon was surreal. His wife had taken their baby and left him and he couldn't fathom why. Russell was certain there was no way Helena could have known about what happened between him and Lucille. It meant nothing to him, but he did regret it. That regret was tinged with shame—shame over how he treated Lucille, and shame he was unfaithful to his wife. The encounter was hardly worth what he had lost. Though serious, he didn't believe his unconfessed infidelity was the cause of Helena's leaving. He loved Russ Jr—as much as Helena would let him—but, ever since Russ Jr came into the world, Helena was a strange creature. He managed to get himself up and walk over to the telephone to dial his in-laws' number.

"Hello," Madeline Wilkes said.

"Momma Madeline, this is Russell."

"Russell. How are you? Did they get off all right?"

"Yes ma'am. Just calling to let you know." *So you already knew they were coming.*

"Thank you, honey. I'm sorry you couldn't come with them. I can't wait to see the baby. You all right? You sound tired."

"Yes ma'am. It's been a rough day."

"Well, you'll have the house to yourself for a few days. You can catch up on your rest," she laughed. "You want to speak to Emmanuel?"

"No ma'am. Tell him hello for me, and I'll catch him later."

"Okay then. I'll tell Helena you called. It'll be late when they get in. You take care. Good bye."

"Yes ma'am." Russell pushed down the button on the cradle and held it in position for a few seconds, then dialed another number.

"Speak," Moses said in his gravelly voice.

"Didn't your mother teach you how to answer a phone?"

"Youngster, what can I do for you?"

"Come over and bring a bottle."

"What? It's a work night and I ain't had my dinner yet."

"Mose, you gotta come. Helena left me."

For a few seconds, there was silence on the other end of the line. "You sure, Youngster?"

"My wife, baby, and a couple suitcases got in a cab and left for North Carolina. Damn right, I'm sure. Just get your ass around here."

"Hold your horses, Youngster. I'm on my way."

Russell hung up the phone and forced himself down the steps to wait for Mose and to find something to eat. Much to his dismay, there was no food on the stove. He grabbed a beer from the refrigerator and some Ritz crackers and a jar of peanut butter from a cabinet. Sitting down at the kitchen table, he sandwiched the gooey stuff between two crackers and popped them in his mouth. The crackers were like dried cardboard and the peanut butter stuck to the roof of his mouth. To wash it down, he took a swig of the beer and, in a fit of anger, swept everything onto the floor. He stared blankly at the fizzing beer bottle until he heard the doorbell ring.

When Russell opened the door, Mose shoved a brown paper bag in his hand and headed for the kitchen. Russell followed.

"Smells like a brewery in here, Youngster. Coulda kept my bottle—" Moses said, before he spied the mess on the floor. "Get a mop and clean this up. You gotta get a grip. Can't be that bad."

161

Russell grabbed a couple of dish towels and half-heartedly swabbed up the beer. "Don't tell me. It is that bad. She just left, just like that," he said, snapping his finger for emphasis. He tossed the dish towels in the sink, took two glasses from the dish rack, and sat down. "What should I do now, Mose?" he said, as he took the Johnnie Walker from the brown bag and poured two shots.

"Let's start from the beginning. I told you, you were ripe for picking. Who you screw?"

"Too bad Helena didn't realize that."

"So, you did get some on the side."

"No. Yes. No. That's not why she left."

"Sounds like a good reason to me. And you can't seem to give up them cards and craps."

"Look, Mose. She just accused me Saturday and was packed and ready to leave today. But she told me that wasn't why she was leaving."

"You told me things weren't right since the baby. Just because she just accused you, don't mean she ain't been thinking it before now. How long you been messin' around?"

"I'm not messing around. I made a mistake. One time. One time. It just happened. There ain't no way she could have known—"

"They always know—"

"That's bull. I think she must have somebody." He dared not tell Mose what he was thinking—*Russ Jr's father*. "That's why she—"

162

"You talk like a fish. You know that woman ain't got nobody else the way she loves you. You the one tomcatting around and trying to blame it on Helena. If you love her and want her back, come clean, beg for forgiveness and ask her to come home. That's all I know."

"That all sounds good, but I need to know why she left in the first place. Something ain't right."

"I can't believe she's gone for good—just like that. That ain't Helena."

"She did say a couple of days—to think about some things—but I don't believe it."

"See—a couple of days. There's hope, Youngster. Do what I told you. Call her and beg."

They talked for a couple of hours, with Russell being alternately angry and anguished. When Mose was ready to leave, reluctantly Russell walked him to the door. The prospect of spending the night in the empty house did not appeal to him. Since he married Helena, they had never spent a night apart.

The walls seemed to close in on him, and as he passed the nursery on his way to bed, he thought he heard the rocking chair and Helena humming. For the first time since he was seven years old, he cried himself to sleep.

♣

The next morning, the jangling of the alarm clock woke Russell from a fitful sleep. Fumbling, he managed to shut it off and pick up the phone. It was 4:30 a.m. and he wanted to let Mose know he wasn't going to work because he needed to do some soul-searching and to figure out how to get his wife back.

Chapter Twenty-seven

Helena regretted telling her father not to pick her up at the train station because she would be late getting in, but there was no way she could have calculated the toll the combination of traveling with a small child and wrestling with inner conflict would take on her mind and body. She was emotionally and physically drained, and her head throbbed.

The station, a small barn-like structure at the edge of town, was devoid of people. Empty. Like her spirit. There was one more stop that night, but the ticket-taker was long gone since there were no scheduled departures until morning. The quiet was occasionally punctuated by the rustling of brown, gold, and orange leaves felled by escaping summer, and by a soft wind whistling through the bare branches of near-by oak trees.

When she was a child, she loved this whistle stop of a station. A visit here meant she was either going off to visit relatives for a vacation, or finally coming home after her nerves were worn thin from enough time with relatives. For now, she just sat on a bench at the cabstand, overwhelmed with how her life was going to change.

Too tired to move from the bench, Helena had waved off two taxis. Peering off into the distance, she heard a squeaking noise and saw a small shadowy figure headed her way. The figure pulled a rickety old black baby carriage by a rope because the handle was broken. At first, she thought she recognized the silhouette and the gait but couldn't quite place it. As the figure came closer, Helena realized it was a woman—Miss Ophelia, who had aged considerably since last she had seen her.

Helena struggled to stand up to greet the old woman. "Miss Ophelia. What in the world are you doing out this time of the night alone, pulling that old baby carriage?"

"Who's asking?" Ophelia said, as she eyed Helena up and down and moved closer.

"Helena. Helena Sinclair... Wilkes."

"Oh, yes. Madeline and Emmanuel's girl. I can ask you the same thing. What *you* doin' out here this time of the night, and with a baby?"

Unconsciously, Helena clutched Russ Jr, cradling him tightly in her arms. "I'm waiting for a taxicab. And you?"

"You know. Business. I came to meet somebody on the train. Trouble. Trouble—" Ophelia muttered and trailed off. "I heard you had a baby. A boy?"

"Yes ma'am."

"Well, some have 'em and don't want 'em. Some want 'em and can't have 'em. People is funny, wouldn't you say?"

"Yes ma'am," replied an uncomfortable Helena.

Ophelia moved closer to Helena. "Let me see your little bundle of trouble, maybe joy."

Helena reluctantly tilted Russ toward Ophelia, and the old woman gently pulled the blanket from around the baby's face.

"Sleepin' peaceful, ain't he? Cute little rascal, but ain't they all at this age. About nine months, give or take a couple of weeks, by my reckoning. Yes? Good size for his age. Where's his daddy?"

"How did you know how old—? Russell is at home—" Helena realized it was more than fatigue that made her want to get out of the train station. She was relieved to hear the sound of a train whistle in the distance.

"Guess the train be here in a few minutes," Ophelia said, more to herself than to Helena. Then she walked into the station without another word, pulling the rickety baby carriage behind her.

167

A taxi pulled up to the stand, and without hesitation this time, Helena hailed it and quickly climbed into the back seat. After the driver loaded her belongings in the trunk, she gave him the address and he headed toward her parents' home.

Just as she suspected, her mother was standing in the picture window waiting for her. As the cab pulled up, her mother rushed to the front door and hurried down the walkway with her husband close behind.

"Helena," an excited Madeline said, as she hugged her daughter and Russ Jr together. "Let me have him, please," she said, taking the baby from Helena.

Emmanuel paid the cab driver and unloaded Helena's things. He kissed Helena on the forehead and headed in the house with her luggage.

"Momma, I didn't want y'all up this time of the night—"

"Don't be silly. We didn't come to the station, but surely you didn't think we'd go to bed before you got here, did you?"

"No ma'am," Helena said, as she dragged herself up the walkway behind her mother who was busy cooing at Russ Jr.

Helena went straight to her old bedroom in the back of the well-appointed rancher where her father had taken her things. Today had been like no other she had ever experienced, and she could hardly wait to get a bath and go to bed. She rooted through her luggage and found a nightgown. *I'll unpack in the morning.*

"Momma, can you keep an eye on Russ Jr while I take a bath?" Before she could hear her mother's response, she closed the bathroom door.

♣

Helena fell asleep as soon as her head hit the pillow. She slept a deep, dreamless sleep while Russ Jr was fast asleep in a crib in her parents' room.

The next morning, she awoke to the smell of bacon and freshly brewed coffee. Donning her robe, she headed to the kitchen where her mother was popping biscuits in the oven.

"Good morning, Momma."

"Morning, honey. How'd you sleep?"

"Peaceful."

"You haven't been sleeping peaceful?"

"No ma'am. I mean, yes ma'am. Poor choice of words, I guess. I was tired, and I feel pretty good now."

"Why so tired? Was the trip that bad?"

"I never travelled with a baby before. I guess that's it. Kinda of mentally tired, too."

"Mentally tired? Sleep wouldn't cure mental fatigue. Don't get me wrong, I'm delighted to see you, but couldn't you have waited until Russell could come with you?"

"I didn't want Russell to come with me."

Finished with the biscuits, Helena's mother stopped beating the eggs she had just cracked into a bowl and stared at Helena. "Why not? What's going on with you two? Is he gambling again?" Madeline put down the wire whisk she was holding and sat down next to Helena.

"Sometimes, but that's not it. He may be seeing somebody."

"Seeing somebody? Russell? I know it's not above most men, but I didn't think that of Russell. Are you doing due diligence? I know sometimes after a baby—"

"We lost something after the baby, and Russell doesn't bond with the baby." She chose her words carefully, so as not to indict herself. Then Helena started sobbing. Truth is she didn't want Russell to get attached to a child that was not his, nor did she want her husband to suspect Russ Jr was not his biological child.

"What is Russell saying?"

"He's angry of course, but I didn't give him time to talk much and I didn't want to talk. I mean, I only brought up the affair the day I left. I had to leave."

"You had to leave? I don't understand. You need to talk to your husband. You don't just up and leave and take his child without talking it out. Doesn't sound like you. Like I said, sometimes after a baby, it takes time for things—you know what I mean—to get back to normal."

"Yeah, I know, but there's the matter of the other woman. I had to leave. I couldn't be intimate with Russell—"

"That's what I mean. Is it really another woman, or you not doing wifely duties?"

"Momma, please—" Helena was so choked up, she started sobbing again. "It's the baby—Russ Jr. Russell doesn't make time for him. He doesn't bond with him."

"Which is it honey? The baby? Another woman? "I don't understand why you didn't talk to Russell about whatever it is."

"Couldn't."

"What do you mean couldn't? Why not? I can't believe you didn't talk to him."

After a long pause, Helena took a deep breath and spoke in a whisper. "Russell may not be Russ Jr's father."

Madeline took Helena by the shoulders and shook her as she fought to keep her voice down. "What do you mean: Russell may not be his father? You mean to tell me, Russell does have reason to act the way he does toward the baby? Just because you think he's having an affair, doesn't give you permission to cut out on him. Two wrongs don't make a right. Your father and I didn't raise you to be a hussy."

"No ma'am," Helena stammered. "How could you think that about me? That's not it. It's because I didn't know—don't know—how to tell him I was assaulted—raped."

Madeline starred at Helena with her mouth and eyes wide open. Barely able to speak, she whispered, "Raped? Raped? Oh my God, child. Are you all right? How could you not tell him? Did you call the police? When did it happen? Who was it? Where did it happen?"

Madeline got up from her chair slowly and started for the kitchen door. "Emman—"

Helena quickly grabbed her arm. "No, Momma. Don't call Daddy. I can't face him with this. I didn't call the police. I mean, they wouldn't take the word of a colored girl over a white man, especially since he was in my house. And that's why Russ Jr is so light."

Slowly, Madeline dropped back into her chair. "A white man? Your house? What was a white man doing in your house?"

"It was the insurance man—at least he was supposed to be an insurance man. Once, I tried to contact him at his office but nobody had heard of him."

"I don't understand why you didn't call the police. Why didn't you at least tell Russell?"

"I just couldn't. Besides that was the day Mose called me from the hospital to tell me Russell was going to lose his hand if they didn't admit him. He hadn't hurt it the way he first told me. I had to rush to the hospital. I was traumatized and confused. I didn't have time to call the police or anything. Worrying about Russell, I tried to put it behind me. Anyway, there is the problem of his cheating, too.

"Adultery is serious, but I think you have a bigger problem. You should have called the police. Now it's about ten months later. My God, child. What did you do?"

"What did *I* do? Nothing. I did nothing! Russell's never going to touch me again."

"That's nonsense. Russell is a reasonable man. You should have told him or gone to the police. You didn't answer my question. What was the man doing in your house?"

"I told you, he was my insurance man. I had no reason to think he would do something to me." But she remembered she always thought he was creepy. "Momma, please. I don't know what to do. I don't think Russell will ever want me again if he knew."

Neither of them heard Emmanuel as he walked into the kitchen. "I'm afraid you might be right, Daughter."

"How long have you been standing there?" Madeline asked.

"Long enough." I hate to say this but, speaking as a man, I think it would be very difficult to be intimate with a wife who has been violated by another man. That would be a hard pill to swallow."

Indignant, Madeline stood up and pointed her finger at her husband. "You mean to tell me you would abandon me if I were assaulted. How dare you!"

"Understand this, please. I would have compassion for you, take care of you, and even try to find the SOB and kill him, but I believe it would take a while before our relationship could get back to normal. I've heard other men say the same thing."

"What men? Where? The barber shop? That's what you talk about in men's bible study? I thought you were a better man than that, Emmanuel. I can't believe you. You need to get out of my sight right now."

"Try to understand where I'm coming from."

"Leave Emmanuel! Just go someplace."

Emmanuel threw up his hands, turned and walked out of the kitchen. A few seconds later, Helena and Madeline heard the front door close.

"Momma, what am I going to do?"

"I wish I knew, but Ecclesiastes says there is nothing new under the sun so I know the answer is in the Word."

"Yes ma'am. I believe that, but—"

Madeline raised her hand to momentarily stop Helena, and then cocked her head as if listening to something. "Seems you father didn't go far."

"Huh? I didn't hear anything."

"Maybe not—I thought I heard the door again."

After a heavy silence, Helena remembered the baby was unattended. "I'd better go get Russ Jr before he starts howling for breakfast."

She walked the short distance to her mother's bedroom and went to the crib. There were crumpled blankets, but no Russ Jr.

"Momma, why would Daddy take Russ Jr with him in his state of mind?"

"What?" Madeline asked, as she entered the room. "I thought he went straight out the door. They must be on the porch."

The two women went out of the house to the front porch. No Emmanuel. No Russ Jr.

"He didn't even wrap my baby up. What was he thinking?" Helena said frantically, as she headed toward the street.

"Calm down, honey," Madeline said, as she followed Helena to the sidewalk. "He probably took the baby with him for a walk." But the car was gone.

"Momma, Daddy didn't go for a walk—." Helena's voice trailed off as she headed up the street, yelling, "Daddy!" while her mother headed down the street, yelling, "Emmanuel!"

When Helena reached the intersection, she heard the eerie screeching noise she had heard at the train station. She quickly turned and headed toward the sound coming from behind a neighbor's holly bush. To her fear and apprehension, Miss Ophelia appeared pulling the beat-up black baby carriage like a horse in a harness. The muffled sounds of a baby crying competed with a music box playing Brahms Lullaby.

Helena rushed to the carriage and forcefully put her hand in Miss Ophelia's chest, yelling, "Stop, old lady! Stop. Momma, call the police."

Helena lifted Russ Jr from the carriage and drew him protectively to her breast. Miss Ophelia had wrapped him in a dirty blanket, but he appeared otherwise unharmed. As Madeline made her way back to the house, a car screeched to a halt near Helena. The driver, a young woman, jumped out, leaving the motor running and the door open. She rushed toward Helena with fear in her eyes. "Helena, please don't call the police. I'll take care of it."

"Beverly? Is that you? Yes, I'm calling the cops. Your mother is dangerous and needs to be committed."

"I know. We're working on it, but she's not dangerous. She's just old and senile. In two weeks, she'll be in a nursing home and will get the care she needs. All the police will do is hand her over to us. Please Helena, for an old friend, I beg you, don't call the police."

"She is not too senile to take my baby from my parents' house. How did she do that? Why did she do that? She's dangerous, I tell you."

"I promise you, nothing else is going to happen. The baby is okay, right?"

Miss Ophelia stopped humming her out-of-tune accompaniment. "The baby be just fine. He just wants to see his daddy. And here, take this. I bought it for him," and with that she handed Helena a small round mirrored music box, which she reluctantly took. On the lid, a ballerina twirled to Brahms Lullaby.

Helena turned to Beverly, and said, "Take her, but if anything else happens, I *will* call the police."

Beverly took her mother by the shoulders and started to lead her to the car. "Thank you, Helena. I'm so sorry. Life hasn't been kind to my mother."

"Really?" Madeline mumbled under her breath. "and your mother hasn't been kind to life. Karma's a bitch."

Beverly ignored Madeline, put her mother in the car, folded the dilapidated baby carriage, threw it in the trunk, and sped off.

As she watched Beverly leave, Madeline beckoned to Helena. "Come on. Let's get inside and make sure Russ Jr is all right. What did she give you?"

"A music box. It's playing something that's familiar, but I don't know where I heard it."

"Looks new. I guess you were too young to remember, but it's playing Brahms Lullaby. Madeline started singing. "'Lullaby and good night, close your little eyes tight. Lay your head on mother's breast like a birdling in its nest. Lay thee down now and rest, may thy slumber be blessed. Lay thee down now and rest, may thy slumber be blessed.' I used to sing it to you when you were a baby."

"You did?"

"Yes, I did. I'm sure you don't remember."

As the two women entered the house, Madeline looked around. "Still no Emmanuel, but I guess he hasn't been kidnapped."

177

At first, the women looked somberly at each other, and then had a much-needed laugh.

♣

It was late afternoon when Emmanuel returned home. Madeline didn't let on how worried she had been, but she asked, "So, where have you been all day?"

"What do you care? You told me to go someplace and that's what I did."

"Let's not do this. You upset me, and I'm still upset—"

"I'm sorry. I didn't mean too, but I had to tell you my feelings. Maybe in a real situation, which I never hope to experience—I would think differently. Anyway, we need to help our daughter figure this out. I sought solace with Rev. Brewington this afternoon, and it helped me. I didn't talk specifics. I'm sure he'll be willing to talk with Helena if she wants to. After all, he watched her grow up. Can you forgive me?" he said with outstretched arms.

Madeline walked into his embrace. "You know how to lay it on thick, don't you? Yes, but we have to talk about it some more. And I need to tell you about Miss Ophelia."

"What's that old witch done now?"

"You'll be shocked, but a little later for that. Don't you think we need to pull out the album for Helena?"

"Yeah, we knew this day would come."

Chapter Twenty-eight

Helena was a jumble of emotions. On one hand, she was glad that she had ridded herself of her horrendous secret, but her stomach still churned knowing Miss Ophelia had kidnapped her baby. She shuddered remembering she had once thought Miss Ophelia was the answer to her problem. The irony of the situation was chilling. Then she dreaded to think of what would become of her marriage, especially if Russell felt the way her father did.

Despite how hurtful her father's earlier words had been, he still had a calming effect on her. As a child and even as a young woman, she always felt he could fix everything from a broken wagon to a broken marriage. She trusted he would fix this situation too. He had called a family meeting for after she had calmed down from the morning's travails. With Russ

Jr down for his afternoon nap, Helena walked into the living room where her parents were seated on the sofa. Her father had an old leather-bound picture album on his lap. He patted the spot between himself and his wife and encouraged Helena to sit with them.

"Daughter, you know you should come to your mother and me at the first sign of trouble, but you didn't. Too late to cry over spilled milk, but I think we can help a little bit. I still may go to Baltimore to see the police—but that's a different matter."

"I don't know, Daddy. What do you think you can do? What's up with the album?"

"Just wait a minute, honey. Your mother and I knew this day would come. We should have dealt with it sooner," Emmanuel said, thumbing through the album. Finding the page he wanted, he pushed the book toward Helena. "Here. Take a look at these pictures."

Helena stared at the photo of a man and woman, then cast a quizzically look, first at her mother, then back to her father. "Who are these gypsy-looking, mafia-looking people, and why do you have these pictures? I never saw them before."

"There's a reason for that," Madeline said. "Those are your father's mulatto grandparents. You know your father's brother the family never talks about—well, that's because he's passing and he cut all ties with his family. They say when he left, he said he would never have children because he was afraid they would look colored."

"Your father was the darkest of his siblings—and he ain't too dark." Madeline chuckled, breaking her own rule on properly spoken English. "Anyway, seems you have the reverse situation—your child looks white. Of course, our babies are always born lighter than they end up being, but Russ Jr's light complexion comes from his grandfather's genes. You need to get on that telephone and call your husband. Maybe you should go home and work this out. Your father and I can keep Russ Jr for a few days."

"Why didn't you tell me about daddy's grandparents before now?"

"No need. Family secrets. All families have them, but they come out one way or another. Your father and I should have told you, and it would have saved you some heartache. If what you say about Russell and the baby is true, you may be right. He's thinking the baby isn't his, but this should ease his mind."

Emmanuel closed the album. "I'll talk to Russell if you want me to. Maybe he should come down here."

Hesitantly, Helena replied, "No, I'll call Russell when I think he's home from work and tell him I'll be coming home—" Her voice trailed off.

"Okay," her father responded, "but let's leave the other matter alone. Let sleeping dogs lie."

"Yeah, another family secret."

Chapter Twenty-nine

Russell fought the urge to go to the Oasis where he felt sheltered and safe in the cocoon of the dark booth in the back of the bar. Even the Lucille incident was far from his mind. He just wanted to get out of the house. He paced the living room and tried to will the hands on the clock, to move to the time when Mose would be home. Finally, he collapsed on the sofa and dropped off to sleep. An hour later he was awakened by the simultaneous ringing of the phone and pounding on the front door. He stretched and decided to answer the phone first, but he didn't reach it before the caller hung up. Shrugging, he headed for the door.

"Mose. You ugly son-of-a-gun. You don't know how glad I am to see you."

"I can get this abuse at home. I came to help you solve your problem, and this is what I get?"

"Excuse my manners. Come on in. You still ugly."

Mose stepped into the living room and threw his jacket in the direction of where an armchair had been, but it hit the floor. He left it there and took a seat on the sofa. "I forgot Helena moved the furniture around. Anyway, word on the street is you have a thing with Lucille, and Nipper is as mad as a wet hen."

"I don't care about the word on the street."

"Okay but consider this a warning. Your problem is, you don't believe bull horns will butt."

"Thanks, but I don't need the down-home wisdom now. What do you think I should do about Helena?"

"You been home all day and you ain't figured that out yet? I told you to call her. Did you do that?"

"No, but—"

"Youngster. Why not? Never mind. You need to get on a train, a bus, or the first thing smokin' and get to North Carolina. I'll take you to the station. I'm not your personal banker, but do you have money?"

"Yeah, just enough."

"Go on get an overnight bag. I ain't got all day."

"I think I need to talk to her first and leave in the morning."

"Suit yourself but do something. If you got it together, I'll head on home."

Russell patted Mose on the back and walked him to the door. "Thanks Mose. You're the best friend a colored man could have."

Mose just shook his head and went down the steps.

♣

Russell couldn't leave well enough alone. He felt lucky: lucky enough to work things out with Helena while increasing the money in his pocket at a quick poker game. He loved her more than life itself, but gambling was the seducer.

After scrounging for something to eat in the refrigerator, Russell grabbed a jacket and headed out the door. Just as he was about to close the front door, he heard the phone ringing, but decided not to answer it. He slammed the door and headed for Pennsylvania Avenue.

The Starlite Club—and many of its patrons—was lit up, inviting early week revelers to dance, flirt, and get drunk. Russell took the alley to the back of the club and knocked.

"Who is it?" came a familiar voice.

"It's me, Scottie. Russell Sinclair."

"Sinclair. You sure you want to be here?"

"Just let me in Scottie. You mind the door and I mind my own business."

Scottie opened the door and directed Russell to the poker game in a room filled with cigarette smoke, stale air, and the smell of sweat and Old Spice.

Russell spotted the usual gang of gamblers and found a place at their table.

Nipper worked the room, momentarily disrupting the players with small talk. He stopped by Russell's chair and whispered in his ear, "You sure you want to be here tonight, Sinclair? You can't afford to lose. You still in debt, boy."

"Yeah. Tonight's the night I balance the books."

Chuckling, Nipper summoned the flirtatious barmaids—one of which was Lucille—to take drink orders as he encouraged the players to ante up. Russell though it best to be as nonchalant as possible, but it did not matter: Lucille completely ignored him.

As she exited the room, she whispered something in Nipper's ear. He stuck a toothpick in his mouth and nodded. Russell didn't miss the encounter, and for a split second was bothered by it, but quickly returned his attention to Five Card Draw and his unsubstantiated belief that his luck was about to change.

Apparently, Russell and Lady Luck had not communicated and she forgot to show up. He folded after losing the hundred and fifty dollars he came with, added to the hundred dollars he already owed the house. At least he had the presence of mind to leave his North Carolina bus fare at home and ignore the urging of the players to stay a little longer because his luck was bound to change.

After he left the table, Russell made his way to the tiny bathroom near the exit. When he came out of the stall, Scottie was blocking the door. The small space put Russell squarely in Scottie's face.

"Outta the way, Scottie," Russell said, attempting to reach around the washed-up pugilist.

"Didn't balance them books, did you? So Nipper wants me to work out your payment plan."

"Oh, so now you're Nipper's accountant too? I didn't think you could count past ten."

"See that's what's gonna get your ass cut. I might have to make an example of you anyway. You don't pay your bills on time."

"I'll handle my business with Nipper, so move."

As Russell attempted to push Scottie away from the door, Scottie pulled out his switchblade. It clicked as somebody banged on the door.

"Somebody fall in in there? I gotta pee," came the voice on the other side of the door. "Open the door!"

Russell took the opportunity to give Scottie a hard shove and he fell sideways against the sink, but not before his elbow caught Russell in the mouth. Russell pushed passed the man at the door and rushed out of the club.

Russell quickly made his way home, finally acknowledging to himself that he was the fool he didn't want to be. And if he didn't get his act together, he could end up dead in an alley some place. It was rumored Nipper had killed or had a delinquent debtor killed for lack of timely payment. Russell didn't want to find out if it was true.

Once at home, he showered, iced his fat lip, and went to bed. Unlike the night before, he fell asleep quickly.

At 5:00 a.m. Russell was awakened by an irritating jangling noise he couldn't identify. *Thought I didn't set that alarm,* he mumbled, while smashing the clock's off button. The jangling persisted until he realized it was the telephone.

"Hello?"

"Russell, what took you so long to—?"

"Helena is that you? Anything wrong—?"

"I called you a couple of times yesterday. No answer. Thought I'd catch you before you went to work. You don't sound right."

"You woke me up outta a deep sleep, that's why," he said, massaging his swollen lip. "I miss you."

"Apparently not much since you were out last night."

"That's because you weren't here. Didn't want to be home by myself. Is everything all right—the baby? You picked a hell of a time to call to fuss. I mean—"

"I didn't call to fuss, Russell. I was calling to tell you I would be home Thursday to talk, but maybe that's not a good idea after all."

Russell bolded upright in bed. "Yes, it is! I was going to come down there. Please Helena. We need to talk."

"You were coming down here? You still sound like you have a mouth full of mush."

"Yeah. You never talked to me on the phone at 5:00 o'clock in the morning. Helena, just come home. I miss you. I love you. I need you."

"Baby's fine. I miss you, too. I'm leaving Russ Jr here, so we won't be distracted. I'll see you Thursday, God willing."

"Blow me a kiss."

♣

After the phone call, Russell walked to the closet and retrieved a small wooden box from the top shelf. He carried it to his bed, brushed the dust off, and reverently rubbed the top. After a pause, he lifted the lid and took out a gold pocket watch that belonged to his late grandfather. In order to get out of Nipper's debt and the influence that relationship had on his marriage, he'd have to sell it. Just thinking about parting with it was painful, but he knew he caused his own pain. Since he wasn't expected at work, he planned to tidy up the house, take the watch to the pawn shop, and find Nipper to settle his debt.

Old habits—bad or good—die hard. Despite the promises he had made to himself, Russell couldn't resist stopping in the Oasis for a quick burger later that day. Since he was not a lunchtime patron, he did not know who was on duty, but he did not expect to see Lucille. He was seated in his favorite booth when she appeared.

"Since ain't nobody here but me, I gotta wait on you. What do you want, bulljiver?"

"Look, I said I was sorry. It shouldna happened that way."

"What way should it have happened?"

"I mean, it should have never happened. I'm sorry—"

"You sure? A word from me and I can keep Nipper off your ass, but I have to get something in return."

"Naw. Thanks, but no thanks. I'm not playing this game with you."

"You don't know what you're missin', Russell. I saved you from a beat down from Scottie the other night after you lost all your money. We can keep it on the down low. Nipper accused me of being sweet on you, but he don't really care and he'll lay off if I tell him to. I just need a little bit of your time, baby."

"Like I said, thanks, but no thanks. I'll settle with Nipper first hand. Now excuse me. I lost my appetite." With that, he slid out of the booth and walked out.

Chapter Thirty

Since she was going home, Helena did not pack a bag, she only took her parent's picture album—the presumed answer to her marital discord. Though she had only been gone three days, home seemed an eternity away. As the bus made its way north, she nodded and turned over and over in her mind what she would say to Russell.

The Greyhound pulled into the station on Eutaw and Center Streets, and the passengers gathered themselves to leave the bus. Hesitantly, Helena left her row and was bumped by a couple of riders who were more focused on exiting than she was.

When she got off, instead of hailing a cab, she looked for the nearest phone and dialed a number.

"Hello," came the voice on the other end.

"Hello Natalie. I'm home."

"Home! Home?"

"Yes, well no. Not Walbrook Avenue home, but at the Greyhound station."

"Why did you leave without telling me? Why did you come back? Tell me something."

"I came back to see if I can patch things up with Russell."

"If you don't, I'll never get married and it will be all your fault."

"You are so dramatic. I'll talk to you tomorrow."

"You need me to come get you?"

"No, I'll get a hack. See ya."

The call to Natalie was just a ruse to postpone the inevitable. Reluctantly, she hailed one of the unlicensed hacks and climbed in. The trip home was a quick one. When she got out of the car and walked up the steps to the house, she hesitated at the front door. Finally turning her key in the lock, she walked across the vestibule into the living room to find Russell standing in the middle of the room. Neither spoke for a few seconds.

Helena fought the urge to run into his outstretched arms, but just spoke instead.

"Hi," they both chorused, then laughed nervously.

"Glad you're home, baby. I missed you. Can I get a hug?"

Ignoring the question, Helena sat on the sofa and patted the spot next to her. "I missed you, too. Who is she, Russell?"

"Whoa! Just like that? No time for niceties, huh? Don't you want some water or want to go to the bathroom or something? I told you, there ain't no she."

"You're lying."

"So that's how we're going to work this out?" He took her hands. "There is, was, nobody. I swear on my mother's grave. Look, the Saturday before you left—I don't know how to say this—I'm so sorry, but I did have ugly, vengeful, meaningless sex with a woman."

Helena snatched her hands back, clasped them over her ears and jumped up from the sofa, screaming, "I don't want to hear it!"

Russell grabbed her by the shoulders. "Either you want the truth or you don't. I know it's hard to hear. It's hard for me to admit it, but I'm coming clean. I'm sorry. I can't say it enough, please forgive me. It meant nothing. I was so mad at you. You had me wound tight."

Helena broke free. "Now it was my fault you screwed another woman? How could you disrespect me like that? How could you, Russell?"

"I'm asking you to forgive me. I was wrong, wrong. You shut me out—I know that's not an excuse—but can you forgive me, please?"

"How dare you come home to me after you violated some woman."

"Violated? She was a willing participant. You make it sound like I took her against her will or something. Willing or not, I was wrong. I'm sorry. I don't know any other way to say it."

"*You* used the word 'vengeful.' That's a strange word to describe screwing, don't you think? I hope it's nobody I know."

"Believe me. It will never ever happen again."

"What will Natalie say?"

"Natalie? What's she got to do with it? I know she's your friend and I love her too, but she ain't got a damn thing to do with this. Besides, there ain't nothing to tell. Look I'm even through with gambling."

"I wish I could believe that."

"If you're not going to believe anything I say, why did you come back home? I'm through with Nipper. I don't owe him nothing. Paid up. Finished."

"How did you do that? Rob Peter to pay Paul? Mose?"

"No. I worked it out. Helena, please. Meet me halfway. I love you. Give me a chance to prove myself."

Russell wrapped his arms around Helena. She tried to free herself, but he wouldn't let go. And in spite of her pain and anger, her body softened in the arms of the man she loved with all her being. After a few seconds, he released her, and she sat back down on the couch.

"I don't know. I didn't know I could hurt so bad. I need some more time. And what about Russ Jr?"

"What about him? You always act like you don't want me around him. Why's that?"

Now it was her turn to be on the defensive and she didn't know what to say, but her father's hurtful words: "...*difficult to be intimate with a wife who has been violated by another man*" and "*let sleeping dogs lie,*" rang in her head.

"Over protective, I guess. Hormones? I dunno." Before the trip to North Carolina, she projected her guilty knowledge onto him and shielded the baby from Russell.

"Sit down Russell. I want to show you something." She picked up the album from the coffee table where she had placed it and thumbed to the page with the pictures of her great grandparents and her father's siblings. She put the book on Russell's lap. "Look at these."

Russell gave the pictures a cursory look. "Okay, but why? Who are they, and why do I have so see them now?"

"They're Daddy's grandparents."

"Strange looking, but so what?"

"Look at them. Daddy has a brother and sister passing for white."

This time he took a closer look. "What? You're lying. But I'm confused. Why did that even come up? What's that got to with our situation?"

"When I told them how you interacted with the baby, they thought you may have thought—how can I say this—that Russ Jr wasn't yours."

"What? That was all you. I don't get it. Did I ever say that or give you any reason to believe I thought that? You knew better, so why did they pull out these pictures? Unless you needed to prove something to yourself. What's going on?"

"In my confused mind, I thought that was what you were thinking, especially the times you looked at Russ Jr strangely. I wanted to protect him." *What a tangled web we weave.*

"Never thought I'd say this, but you sound like a crazy woman." *Fess up. You did have some doubts.* "So Pop Emmanuel has some half white ancestors, and my son got the genes. I be dammed!"

"Where are we now, Russell?"

"Wish I knew. I'm tired. This back and forth is wearing me out and giving me a headache. I need a bath and some rest. We can talk some more in the morning. I gotta take this in." With that, he headed toward the steps. "If you're hungry, I have a little pocket change—*real pocket watch change.* "You can go to the Chinee joint and get something."

"Nothing here, huh? We're not finished—okay. Let me freshen up a bit." She held back the tears as she walked on wobbly legs upstairs to the bathroom.

They barely said a word to each other for the rest of the evening and purposely avoided the elephant in the room.

♣

The next morning, still half asleep, as was her habit, Helena patted the right side of the bed, but did not find Russell there. Then she remembered she had relegated him to the spare bedroom until she sorted things out.

She slid out of bed and walked down the hall to peep into the small room. Vacant. Russell had gone to work. Disappointed and conflicted, she went back to her bed. By punishing Russell, she was depriving herself of the very thing she enjoyed most about marriage—intimacy and affection from the man she loved. Could she forgive him for his infidelity? The Bible said she should, but she felt like she was violated, not just by Evan Monahan, but by her husband as well. He had promised in front of a church full of people, to forsake all others and to be faithful to her, but he broke his promise. Since she could not go back to sleep, she went to the kitchen to make herself some coffee.

The ambivalence and separate sleeping arrangement continued for a week when her mother called to tell her it was time to get her baby. She even offered to send a bus ticket which Helena readily accepted. She told her mother she and Russell had not completely worked out their problems, but she thought they would. When she told Russell she was going to get the baby, he begged her not to stay in North Carolina.

During the week, she and Russell had many discussions, many of them heated and hurtful. Helena had finally accepted the fact that Russell's infidelity lacked emotional involvement, but the fact that it was so recent was difficult for her to digest. As for the matter of Russ Jr's paternity, she believed the issue was settled and she never intended to tell Russell about the rape.

Chapter Thirty-one

February 1957...

A month later, things at the Sinclair house were almost normal. There were times when Helena had to force herself not to recoil at Russell's touch. He didn't deserve an unresponsive wife. Most times, she was able to mask it, but when she couldn't, she knew he assumed it was a reaction to his infidelity.

Russell confided in Mose who insisted he give it more time. And he did. Since his assignation with Lucille, Russell rarely visited the Oasis unless he knew Lucille was off, and never the Starlite Club. Occasionally, he ran into Natalie. He didn't know whether or not it was her job to spy on him because she didn't leave, as was her old habit, when she found him in the same club.

But as was his custom, he made a fatal error. He heard through the grapevine Lucille had been badly beaten by her boyfriend—he assumed Nipper—and was in the hospital. He thought the least he could do to apologize for his past behavior was to send her some flowers. After all, he had known her for quite some time. He stopped at Bonaparte Florists and sent Lucille an inexpensive bouquet with a simple 'Get well soon,' note, signed 'R. Sinclair.' Without a second thought, he stuck the receipt in his pocket.

♣

Natalie parked her car on the small hospital lot and headed for the entrance to Provident Hospital. *I don't know why I'm going to see this woman; she's not one of my favorite people. I don't even know her last name. Good thing I have the room number, or I'd be embarrassed at the information desk.*

Natalie took the elevator up to the third floor and found room 305. She went in slowly.

"Hey, Lucille. How you doing? Dumb question, huh?"

Lucille's left arm was in a cast and her face was badly swollen. As Natalie walked toward the bed, she saw the surprise in Lucille's eyes.

"Yeah. You the last person I expected to see. You trying to make up for yo' nasty ass attitude?" Lucille managed to say, out of the side of her mouth.

"True, we're not best buds, but I've known you—well sort of—for a long time and I just thought—"

"Thanks, but it sounds like bullshit to me. I haven't had a run on bar patrons coming to see me."

"Okay. My mistake. Sorry I came." Natalie started to back out of the room. "Somebody loves you, though. You have nice flowers."

"Mostly from Nipper, trying to make up. Oh, and one from your boy, Russell."

"Russell? That's nice. Not my boy," Natalie said, trying to sound noncommittal.

"I just figured it out. You want him for yourself? Uh-huh! Don't know why I never figured it out."

"You're crazy, Lucille. That's my girl's man and I was just looking out for her. I don't do underhanded crap like that. But you better lay off."

"Hell, you say."

"Yeah, I say. See you, Lucille. Get well—or don't." With that, Natalie rushed out of the room and to the elevator. She chastised herself as she got into the car. *Natalie, why did you do that? What was the point?*

♣

Come wash day, Helena was going through Russell's pockets, a routine act, only to find the receipt from the florist. Helena was livid, red hot. *So he's sending flowers to that skank, Lucille. Is that who he's been fooling with? And he said it meant nothing. A one-time mistake? Yeah right.*

The anger gave way to pain and oddly, relief. Helena had a deep-seated need to make Russell look bad to assuage her own misplaced guilt. She left Russ Jr with Aunt Loretta so she would be ready for Russell when he came home.

As soon as Russell unlocked the door and stepped into the vestibule, Helena attacked. "So Lucille, the barmaid, is the heifer you've been screwing?"

Taken aback, Russell just stood there, mouth agape. "What the hell are you talking about? Something that's six months old?"

"The flowers, Russell. Why are you sending that skank flowers?"

Russell sat on the sofa, dirty clothes and all, and let Helena rant without saying a word. When she was spent, he quietly told her the whole story from beginning to end, to include how he felt about himself, the gambling, the beatings he had taken, and how the one time encounter with Lucille bordered on an assault. After he finished talking, Helena looked at him in amazement. She was in shock.

"As soon as I take a bath, I'll pack a few things and leave, okay?"

Flabbergasted, Helena shouted, "No, you can't leave! I don't want you to leave."

"What do you want then? I'm tired of walking on egg shells. Nervous about which Helena I'm sleeping with. I think you want me gone."

"No, I don't! I just want things to be the way they used to be."

"In that case—" He picked her up—dirty clothes and all—carried her upstairs, dropped her on the bed and told her to stay put while he took a quick bath. When he returned, *things* were the way they used to be. Maybe the flowers weren't a fatal mistake after all.

Chapter Thirty-two

The dynamics of relationships are sometimes confounding, and so it was with Helena and Russell. Strangely enough, after their last major confrontation, the Sinclairs found the magic they had lost. Since it was not economically feasible, Helena did not go back to work. The cost of a babysitter would take most of her meager check, so she stayed home. Since Russell had stopped gambling, they could take in a movie every now and then. Russ Jr was growing like a weed, and father and son had bonded at last. Russell no longer cast a jaundiced eye in the baby's direction.

What Helena did not know was one day when she was at the hairdresser, Russell had rummaged through her hospital records to find her and Russ Jr's blood type. Helena was type 'O' and Russ Jr 'A.' Then one day on his lunch hour, he had gone to the American Red Cross, ostensibly to give blood, but really to find out his own blood type—AB. He remembered the incident well.

The phlebotomist was a plain, average looking young woman and Russell flattered her by giving her a big smile, an appreciative look, and asked her about her day. Then as she prepared him for the procedure, he struck up a conversation.

"Bet you get a lot of these every day."

"A lot of these? What do you mean? People giving blood?"

"Yes, well no. Men wanting to know their blood type."

"Nope. Of course we have to type them, but that's not why they come—they just want to give blood—I think."

"I'm curious. What's my type?"

The young woman looked curiously at Russell then his chart. "You should get an American Red Cross ID card with your type stamped on it, but in the meantime, you're type AB."

"Really? Thanks."

"Mr. Sinclair please be careful with this information and how you use it. Blood typing only eliminates paternity, it doesn't confirm it."

Russell sensed the woman had been asked the question before from other men seeking truth. "Right, I was just curious that's all. Thanks."

In a subsequent trip to the library, Russell found out the father of an A baby and an O mother could only be an A or AB. Because he needed it to, Russell thought the information put the issue to rest.

♣

On this particular evening, Helena was busying herself with a simple Friday meal—pork chops and baked beans—so she and Russell could catch an early movie. WEBB radio was playing Sam Cooke's 'You Send Me' softly in the background and Russ Jr, was in his play pen when she heard someone banging on the front door.

"What's wrong with the doorbell," she muttered, as she went to answer the door.

She caught a glimpse of Mose but could only see the arm and shoulder of the person standing next to him. Looking closer, Helena gauged that it was Clarice. *Funny. Why are they here?*

As soon as she opened the door, she also saw a white man in construction clothes, previously out of sight. She froze and screamed to the top of her lungs. "No! No! Don't tell me!"

Mose grabbed her around the shoulders as she started to slowly sink to the floor. "Let's go inside, Helena."

As soon as they went inside, Helena collapsed onto the sofa. "How bad is it?" she managed to say.

The white man introduced himself as Russell's foreman, John Harper. "I'm sorry to tell you this, Mrs. Sinclair, but there's been a terrible accident and

Russell's been seriously hurt. I'm here to take you to the hospital."

"How bad is it? Somebody tell me!" she screamed, tears streaming down her face.

"Pretty bad," Mose replied with down cast eyes. "Clarice will stay with the baby. Get what you need and let's go."

"What hospital? Russ Jr doesn't know Clarice."

"It'll be okay," Clarice said, as she went to pick up Russ Jr who was wailing in response to the commotion.

♣

When they pulled up to the emergency door at Johns Hopkins Hospital, the sidewalk was lined with construction workers, some of whom appeared to have been crying. John and Mose rushed Helena to the area where Russell had been taken, and a doctor met them outside the exam room.

"Is this Mrs. Sinclair?" he asked, as he took her hand and placed an arm around her shoulder. When John and Mose nodded in the affirmative, the doctor tightened his grip on Helena. "Mrs. Sinclair, we did all we could do. We're sorry for your loss."

With that, Helena fainted. When she was revived, John explained that some scaffolding had collapsed and Russell had been caught under the rubble. Her world had imploded. She was in a daze and felt outside of her body, looking at her disintegrating life. When the doctor took her to see a lifeless Russell, she collapsed onto the gurney, screaming his name. The staff let her cry heart-wrenching tears until there were no more, and then led her to a private waiting room.

After a time, Mose managed to get Natalie's phone number from Helena and asked her to meet them at Helena's house. When they arrived, Clarice had managed to quiet Russ Jr who played; he was untouched by the tragedy that had befallen him and his mother. Natalie called Helena's parents and told them what happened to Russell. They told her they would take the next flight to Baltimore.

Chapter Thirty-three

Helena's worse nightmare had come true. Now she knew what was meant by a self-fulfilling prophecy. She had lost her husband and was now a 25-year-old widow. The pain of her loss was so severe, she did not know how she could go on. It hurt to move, to breathe. It even hurt to think. Save for Russ Jr, she would have given up and died.

She had never gotten another life insurance policy on Russell, so she had to depend on her parents and the kindness of her neighbors and friends to get Russell buried. Even Nipper had the audacity to show up offering help, which Helena summarily refused. Helena's parents had been flabbergasted that she did not have Russell insured. Had they known, they told her they would have bought a policy themselves.

Despite what she knew would be a futile attempt, Helena tried to contact Beneficial Life again by calling the Claims Department number on the back of her premium book. This time, since she wanted to file a claim, the representative was more responsive. After giving the representative her policy number, Helena was told the policy was never in force. Oddly, the representative told her the paperwork was incomplete and had no signatures. She assumed the insurance was cancelled at the customer's request. Insult was added to injury.

Helena took some small comfort in knowing there would be some compensation from Russell's job, but it would be slow in coming. At her father's insistence, she had retained a lawyer who warned her the process could be long.

Given the state of her life, Helena planned to move back to North Carolina with her parents after she emptied the house and got it sold. They said they would pay her way to college if she came to live with them. Though she hated to be dependent, she had reluctantly agreed because she realized it was an opportunity of a lifetime despite the circumstances.

♣

One morning, a month after Russell's funeral, coffee cup in hand, Helena walked to the front door to get the morning paper. As was the custom at the time, a black wreath hung on the door to indicate the household was in mourning. She picked up the paper, made her way back to the dining room and flipped to the local section, which she always read first. The startling headlines made her immediately drop her coffee cup and gasp. Shocked, she was oblivious to the hot coffee that splashed on her leg. The paper read:

Prominent Financier Dies in Private Plane Crash. Son to Take the Helm.

Beneath the headline was a picture of a man of about 65 next to a picture of his son. The father looked vaguely familiar, but she knew the son—Evan Monahan. Helena paced back and forth in the dinner room several times before her eyes cleared enough for her to read the accompanying story:

Prominent insurance tycoon and financier, Connor Monahan III was killed yesterday when his Piper Cub crashed somewhere over upstate New York. Recovery efforts were hampered by last night's severe thunderstorms but resumed this morning.

Connor was the founder and managing director of the Monahan Investment Group, Ltd, which owns a number of banks, investment houses, and insurance companies. His son, Evan Monahan, Chairman of the Board of the North American Beneficial Life and Casualty Insurance Company, is slated to take over the helm of the entire enterprise.

A spokesman at the family's Roland Park home had no comment for the press and asked reporters to honor the family's privacy.

There was more, but Helena thought her head would explode. She could not read any more but continued to stare at the picture of the two men. Evan looked a great deal like his father, except his father had a mole on the left side of his face, above his lip.

Despite her level of incredulity, Helena managed to put together a logical plan in her head. She would bide her time. She scanned the paper every day to find Connor's obituary notice, funeral arrangements and the address of where the family was receiving mourners and accepting condolences.

A week after the services, she took a cab to the Roland Avenue address and walked more confidently than she felt up to the front door. Her nerves were getting the best of her and she jumped when the doorbell chimed. The air left her lungs when a familiar black woman in a gray uniform and white apron opened the door.

"Clarice?"

"Helena?"

"What are you doing here?" they both chorused.

Clarice was the first to speak. "I work here. How come you're here?"

Helena could barely speak. "I'd like to speak to Mr. Evan Monahan."

"Mr. Evan? You have an appointment? What for Helena? I can't believe my eyes, but I'm sorry, they're not hiring. See the wreath on the door? The Monahans are in mourning."

"I know, and I'm not looking for a job. I need to speak to Evan."

"Evan? You can't call—"

In the middle of what she was saying, Evan came to the door, "What is it Ressy?" He looked out and stopped dead in his tracks, his face drained of color.

"This lady, uh, Helena Sinclair, says she wants to speak to you. I told her she couldn't."

"It's all right, Ressy. I'll take her to the Library. You can get her a glass of water."

Helena was dumbfounded and could see the curiosity and confusion on Clarice's face. Evan led the way to the library and motioned for Helena to take a seat in a Louis XIV chair next to the desk. Clarice bought the glass of water, but avoided looking at Helena.

"You can go, Reesy. Make sure you close the door behind you."

"Are you sure?"

"Am I sure? Of course I'm sure. Now excuse us."

After Clarice slowly left the room, Helena took in the opulence of her surroundings: mahogany book selves flanked one wall with an American flag in one corner and a Maryland State flag in the other; a large globe of the earth in a three-legged wooden stand stood in front of a wall where an ornate tapestry hung; and on the wall behind the highly polished desk were framed certificates, awards, and a family portrait. After she had taken it all in, she and Evan stared at each other for a few seconds before she spoke.

"So you're not a lowly insurance collector after all. You're a despicable, perverted man."

"I can see how you would say that Helena, but I meant no harm."

"No harm? No harm? You ruined my life, and I'm going to the police!"

"I know this is hard for you to believe, but I am sorry. Look around," he said with a flourish of his arm. "Do you think the police will believe you over me, especially after all this time? It's your word against mine. After all, you invited me in. I think you were infatuated with me."

"You're a liar. If the police don't believe me, the News American and the Baltimore Sun might find the story quite interesting."

"If they run it. Money speaks loudly."

"And scandal sells papers."

"It goes without saying, but it's a shock to see you. I am sorry, but don't make me play hardball. What do you want?"

"What's rightly mine—my *deceased* husband's life insurance. And by the way, I have an eleven-month old son." Helena fumbled through her purse, pulled out a picture of Russ Jr, and handed it to Evan.

He let out an audible gasp. "What are you saying? I didn't know—"

"Did you care to know? I think the local papers will jump all over this, and it costs money to raise a child."

"Mrs. Sinclair. Helena. Think about what you are threatening to do. It might not turn out the way you think."

"Really?"

"Really. Think about it first. Give me a week to get some legal advice and get back to you."

"Why should I?"

"Because I need to right a horrible wrong. Please give me a week. I am truly sorry for the harm I've caused you."

"I shouldn't let you off the hook that easily, and I don't know why I should trust you, but I do. One week or I'll go to the press and the police. If nothing else, it'll get ugly."

"I know I lied, and worse. But I'll make it right."

"Is that possible? Anyway, one week. I'll show myself out."

"By the way, you and Ressy seem to know each other."

"Yes, we're acquainted. I call her Clarice."

With that, Helena walked out of the library and toward the front door. Clarice met her and walked out with her.

Clarice spoke in hushed tones. "I'm sorry I acted the way I did. I was shocked to see you here."

"Who you telling? You weren't the only one. You never mentioned any names of the people you worked for."

"No need to. Anyway, I hope everything is all right. You know?"

"Why wouldn't it be?

"Sorry, I just hope it isn't what I think—"

"What you think? What *do* you think? Never mind, it's really none of your concern—"

"You're right." Then Clarice hurried back inside.

♣

After Helena left, Evan got up from his chair and went to make sure the library door was closed. When he peered out, Clarice was walking across the foyer. Their eyes locked and Clarice gave Evan a questioning, perplexed look, which he ignored. He slammed the door and went back to his chair. For a long time, he sat quietly in deep thought. *Chickens do come home to roost, don't they? I can't believe she had the audacity to show up here. Ah, but she's still beautiful even with the dark circles under her eyes and the stressed look on her face. I told her I was sorry. Sorry about her husband and sorry about.... Anyway, I am, but I won't be extorted or blackmailed! She doesn't know I'm on the board at the Sunpapers—that story won't see the light of day, but she's right. Could get ugly. Baby? I don't think so. Well Ev, old man, what are you going to do?*

With trembling hands, he picked up the phone on the desk and dialed his best friend's private line.

"Hilderbrandt."

"Hey Chaz. How you doing? Look I need some legal advice."

"Get to the point, why don't you? Hello to you, too."

"Sorry, but I'm desperate and I need confidentiality."

215

"What is it? Illegal or immoral? Remember, as an officer of the court, I will turn your ass in to the nearest policeman or maybe it should be your priest."

"I'm serious. I need some friendly advice and maybe a favor."

"Shoot. What is it?"

"Not on the phone. Can I meet you at your place about eight tonight?"

"Sure. I'll see you then."

Chapter Thirty-four

During the past two days, Helena found herself pacing a lot while waiting for Evan to respond to her innuendoes. To think, she dared threaten a man who had enormous wealth and power. Who knew? To think the creepy insurance salesman was a blueblood member of Baltimore's elite. She was afraid she had been wrong in her approach to the problem, but at the time, it felt like the right thing to do. Now she just had to wait. Wait for what, she didn't know.

Most of the packing was done and the furniture that had not been sold or given away had been shipped to her parents' house. The Salvation Army was scheduled to pick up the remaining items—Russ Jr's play pen and bed, the dinette set, and a folding cot—on the day she was to leave. Natalie would handle issues with the new owners who were scheduled to move in in thirty days.

Nervously sipping her Saturday morning coffee while Russ Jr busied himself in his playpen, Helena thought of Clarice. She simply could not get over the fact that she had worked in the house where the man who raped her lived. How could that be? She wondered if he had ever been improper with Clarice. Suddenly a light bulb went off in her head. Clarice had been a victim, too. Not of Evan, but of his father, Connor III. That's why something about Connor's picture gave her pause. She should have known from the mole above his lip. Raymond. *Connor Monahan III was Raymond's father and Evan was his half-brother. My God! That explains everything. Why she never identified his father. Why he was raised by his maternal grandparents. Rapists. Two generations of rapists. Is that what Clarice meant by 'I hope it's not what I think?'*

Helena put down her coffee cup and started pacing again, wondering what, if anything, she should do about the revelation. She decided to call Clarice, which was what she had been avoiding since their encounter at the Monahans'. She didn't know what to say then and she didn't know what she would say to Clarice now, but she called anyway. Clarice answered the telephone.

"Hello Clarice, or should I say 'Ressy'?"

"It's you. I thought you would call, but don't call me Reesy. I'm Clarice. I can't talk right now."

"I'm sorry. I sure would like to talk to you. When's a good time and where? Maybe here?"

"Okay. Your house will be fine. I can be there in about half an hour."

"Sounds good. See you then."

Helena hung up the phone and took Russ Jr out of his playpen to put him down for his morning nap. She contemplated the situation she was in and wondered what Clarice had to say about it.

True to her word, Clarice arrived at Helena's within thirty minutes. A nervous Helena was at the front window when Clarice parked the car and walked up to the door.

"Thanks for coming, Clarice. Sorry for the house, but you know I'm moving. I have chairs in the kitchen. Come on. Want some coffee?"

"No thanks." Clarice took a seat and went straight to the point. "How do you know Evan?"

"He was supposed to be my insurance man, but I see that wasn't true. He cheated me out of Russell's life insurance."

"Really? His mother never wanted him doin' that, but he said he had to learn the business from the bottom up. I thought he had other reasons. Since his father's death, people seen the newspaper and started comin' to the house looking for a handout. I thought maybe you—"

"Me begging? No! I just wanted what was rightfully mine." She purposely left out the fact that she showed Evan a picture of Russ Jr "You say other reasons. What other reasons? Did he say something after I left?"

"No, but he was upset. What ain't you telling me?"

"Let me ask you the same thing. Tell me about Raymond."

"I guess you figured it out. Connor III is Raymond's father."

"Rape?"

"Yes and no. I thought he loved me. I was young and dumb and lived in their house when my grandmother worked for them. Connor gave me trinkets, money sometimes, took me on trips with him and Miss Maureen. I thought he did it 'cause he loved me and I owed him something in return. Then came Raymond and the relationship ended. Connor started spending most of his time in New York. He put money in a trust fund for Ray's eighteenth birthday, but Ray could only get it if I kept working there. Plus his wife wanted me to stay on. She acted like she didn't know what was going on. What did Evan do to you?"

"I don't know what to say. I'm sorry that happened to you Clarice. Like you say, you were young, but Evan didn't—"

"You're lying."

Helena had not said the words out loud since she told her parents. "You're right. Evan raped me."

"Son of a bitch. I knew it. I guess Russ Jr and Raymond are related."

"Don't be ridiculous. They are not. I just want my insurance money."

"Have it your way. Just be sure you know what you're doing. I gotta go. Mose don't know none of this, so please keep it to yourself."

"That goes both ways. Thanks for coming by."

Helena walked Clarice to the door and they embraced, both women trying to hold back tears.

Clarice paused before she got in the car and turned back to Helena, "I think he named his cat, Lena, after you."

♣

Come Monday, Clarice had reluctantly gone to work. She was hoping to avoid any confrontation with Evan, but she was clearing the breakfast dishes when he came in the backdoor from his morning constitutional. To her chagrin, he had not left for the office.

"Morning, Ressy. Any more coffee?"

Without answering, she poured a cup of coffee and handed it to him. Evan grabbed her wrist.

"Have a seat, Ressy."

Hesitantly, Clarice sat down. "What is it, Evan?"

"What, no 'mister' this morning? Don't forget who you are. Let me get to the point. How do you know Helena Sinclair?"

221

"Frankly, Evan, it ain't none of your business, but if you have to know, Mose and her husband work—worked—together. Helena and I are casual acquaintances. I guess she told you her husband was killed on the job."

"She did mention that. What did she say about me?"

"Why would she say anything about you to me?"

"Just curious." He shrugged his shoulders. "Remember you have a good job here, and mother likes having you around. Doesn't matter to me. I'm going to see Chaz. Thanks for the coffee, *Clarice.*"

With that he got up and left the room.

Clarice was not concerned with Evan's veiled threat about her job especially since her son was his half-brother, but she wasn't sure what would happen to Helena.

Chapter Thirty-five

Helena's constant state of agitation was making Russ Jr cranky and miserable to be around. She knew he sensed his father's absence, and she prayed he didn't hurt like she did. Her pain permeated sinew and bone so deep, it paralyzed her at times and she would drop to her knees. The sooner she got out of the nearly empty house that echoed every sound, reverberated with deep darkness and engulfed her with loneliness, the better off she and Russ Jr would be. Oddly, the one thing that soothed him was Miss Ophelia's *Brahms Lullaby* music box which she fished out of a box of toys and gave to him.

In two days, Evan's week would be up, and she was writing notes for what she would say to the police and the local newspapers. She chewed on her pencil, debating with herself over the ultimatum she had given Evan when the doorbell rang. Before she opened the door, she was taken aback by how good looking the man standing there was. Then she noticed a non-descript Fairlane with 'courier service' painted on the side parked at the curb.

"Can I help you?" she asked.

"Yes ma'am. Special Delivery for Mrs. Helena Sinclair. Is that you?"

When Helena nodded in the affirmative, the courier handed her a plain 8 ½ inch Manila envelope with just her name and address, and pointed to a space at the bottom of a delivery receipt. "Please sign here," he said.

Helena could barely write, her hands shook so much. She thanked the courier, quickly closed the door and ran to the kitchen where she tore open the envelope only to find another envelope and a letter. She read the letter quickly, then out loud and then again slowly. She didn't know if she could trust its contents or even her interpretation of it. Then she tore open the second envelop and stared at its contents for a few seconds. Finally, she danced around the kitchen shouting, "Thank you, Jesus."

That night she slept the best she had in weeks.

Chapter Thirty-six

Helena had finally gotten everything settled with the house. Natalie promised to take care of the morning glories growing in the kitchen window box and would insist the new owners do so as well. They had a tearful goodbye but promised to keep in touch.

Helena had also managed to tuck away some of her painful memories in the deep recesses of her heart, though she missed Russell more than she believed possible. At those times when she felt physical pain thinking about her lost, she would hug or kiss Russ Jr and thank God for him. She knew the pain of losing Russell would be with her forever to some degree, but she was so glad she was blessed with his son. About that—she had no doubt!

Contently, Russell Jr was sleeping on her lap as the Greyhound bus made its way down Route 301 to

North Carolina. Things were not all doom and gloom. A half smile came to her face every time she read the letter she carried with her ever since she received it. The author had painstakingly ensured the letter or its contents could not be traced back to him. The letter read:

My Dear Mrs. Sinclair:

Words cannot express the sorrow I feel for your loss and the pain I have caused in your life. I am sure there is nothing I can do to correct the errors of the past; however, I hope the enclosed cashier's check for $50,000, will help ameliorate some of your suffering.

Please note, Mrs. Sinclair, there will be no further remuneration and you should not attempt to extort more. Information and photos I have received from my investigators confirm what I already knew: the child is not mine and never could have been. I share with you a secret few others know, I have been impotent since I had mumps-induced viral orchitis at age thirteen.

Regards,

An Acquaintance

Helena purposely and carefully refolded the letter and tucked it back into her purse. She laid back on the headrest, closed her eyes, and smiled contently as the bus made its way south.

ACKNOWLEDGEMENTS

Many thanks to two people—Christine Johnson and Sheron Banks Stewart—who constantly pestered me about writing and who were genuinely happy when I put fingers to keyboard.

Thanks also to Joyce Smith and Dorothy Morris for early reading and review. Special thanks go to Dorothy for suggestions that enhanced the plot line and for her editorial skills.

www.ingramcontent.com/pod-product-compliance
Lightning Source LLC
Chambersburg PA
CBHW071314250626
47159CB00004B/1427